The Nanking Cargo

Michael Hatcher
with Max de Rham

The Nanking Cargo

Written by Antony Thorncroft

Hamish Hamilton   London

First published in Great Britain 1987
by Hamish Hamilton Ltd
27 Wrights Lane, London w8 5TZ

Photographs by John Bremmer, Max de Rham and by courtesy of Christie's Fine Art
Design by Gerald Cinamon, Cinamon and Kitzinger

British Library Cataloguing in publication Data

Hatcher, Michael
 The Nanking cargo.
 1. Treasure trove—South China Sea
 I. Title
 622'.19'0924   G525

ISBN 0-241-12117-5

Typeset in 11/14 Linotron Aldus
by Rowland Phototypesetting, London

Printed in Great Britain by
William Clowes Ltd, Beccles, Suffolk

1

At the Last Gasp

Captain Mike Hatcher had had enough. For two months he had been hunting for a wreck, slowly and laboriously combing the waters around the Admiral Stellingwerf Reef, a notorious hazard for shipping in the South China Sea. Along with his partner, Max de Rham, a marine geophysicist, Hatch had invested over £300,000 in the search. At first things had looked promising, the initial investigation of the Reef turning up two old anchors, but after that – nothing.

The days of tedium were beginning to get to Hatch's team of divers. Despite his daily pep talks, concentration was slackening and, more ominously, the weather was threatening to change. It was May 11, 1985; within a month the storms would arrive, making diving conditions very treacherous – had there been anything to dive for.

So Hatch decided to call it a day. On the last of his frequent trips back to Singapore, over a hundred miles away to the north-west and his base, he had telephoned the wives of his team members telling them to expect their husbands in a few days. Now he was packing up the equipment on the barge which he had towed out to sea to provide living quarters during the dive. It was very frustrating. Hatch was the acknowledged expert on marine salvaging in the Far East. Only

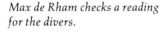

Max de Rham checks a reading for the divers.

eighteen months previously, on that very Reef, he had discovered and successfully salvaged a seventeenth-century Chinese junk laden with porcelain. Now his most ambitious expedition yet had proved a failure. But with costs steadily mounting he could not afford any more "one more day's".

It was Max de Rham who stayed his hand. Max, a friend and former rival, of Hatch, had brought along his sophisticated equipment for the search – the side-scan sonar, which could provide a "map" of the sea bed, and the magnetometer, which detected any ferromagnetic objects lurking at the bottom of the ocean. It was Max's first hunt, and he was reluctant to admit to failure. Hatch is very much a man of action, quickly ground down by routine, but Max has the patience of Job. Over their evening bottle of red wine and game of backgammon, Max asked Hatch for three more days at sea. Although they had covered the most promising area, a stretch of water up to four nautical miles south of the Reef, with no success, a few anomalies had shown up on the sonar just outside the target zone, and even further south. Max wanted an extension.

The Restless M *approaches the barge* (above).

The tower on the reef. From here the survey boat was guided down lines of discovery.

Hatch compromised on two days. To fill the time he went back to dive again on the Reef itself, which, along with most of his team, he still considered the most likely grave of any wreck. Perhaps the old vessel he had his sights on was hidden below one of the many modern ships that had come to grief there? Anyway it would keep his divers busy while Max indulged his fancy.

So it was just another day on the *Restless M*, the converted trawler which was Hatch's home and the nerve centre of the search. The sun shone down piteously as it had done with regular monotony during the whole expedition. Max de Rham was stretched out on the promenade deck reading a French novel between survey lines. It was the turn of Biji, his long-time assistant, to study the side-scan sonar, housed in a tiny cabin. Biji was looking for any unusual dark shapes emerging on the "map". One diver, Hans, was propped up on a tower erected on the Reef, directing the sweep of the boat, while another diver, Dorian, was trying to concentrate at the long drop station where less and less frequently he was asked to release the buoy which would mark a spot which was worth investigating.

Suddenly, just after noon, the sonar became very interesting. Unaccountable images appeared and there were odd deep holes,

The tell-tale evidence. The shapes that told Max he might have found a wreck (left). The sonar at work (below).

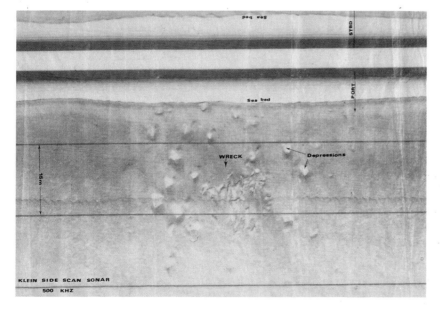

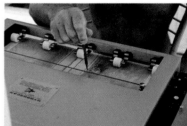

apparently on the sea bed. At the same time the magnetometer started clicking away like crazy, suggesting that magnetic objects were scattered around in an area one hundred and thirty feet in length – an exciting design.

Checking out the sonar print run.

"Drop," shouted Max, and Dorian let go of the buoy. *The Restless M* made a slow semi-circle and stopped.

Discussion started: should they trail over the area again, or trust that the buoy was close enough to the "find"? Anyway it was promising enough to call Hatch over from the Reef.

Secretly Max was very excited but he did not want to raise Hatch's spirits too high: there had been enough disappointments. The two men quickly kitted themselves up in their diving gear, got into the dinghy and sped over to where the buoy was bobbing around. Into the water they went, Hatch first. By pulling themselves down on the line stretching from the marker buoy to its anchor they quickly reached the ocean bed, one hundred and twenty feet below. It was grey and featureless down there, and they needed to use their compass to swim towards the first of those strange depressions.

It turned out to be a hole, six feet wide and five feet deep. Max dived in, down to the bottom. A Moray eel scuttled out of his way but he hardly noticed it – emerging from the cloud his prodding hands had created in the cavity was a small white encrusted coffee cup. Max gathered it up and swam towards Mike who had taken another direction. He had made towards a shoal of fish – snappers and groupers – well aware that such a concentration of fish is a good indication of a wreck. As Max tried to attract Hatch's attention, both men swam slap-bang into a brick wall. They eyed each other in wonder. What had they found – was it a modern wreck? Soon their questions were answered. Close to the partially collapsed wall was a massive anchor, the twin of the one found on the Reef.

The two men had arrived at an under-water oasis, alive with fish and coral. They had little time to admire the scenery. Much more interesting to them was the sight of cannon, lying in profusion at all angles. Hatch started to dig around the cannon and came across some jagged objects. But by now their dive time was almost exhausted. Reluctantly they made for the surface, Hatch clutching his odd shapes, Max his complete coffee cup.

As the anxious divers gathered around them, Hatch rubbed away the accumulated marine growth and the broken objects came up gleaming blue and white: it was porcelain. Hatch was back in business.

No-one had any idea of the identity of the wreck or the contents of the cargo. More to the point, it was odds-on that any merchandise had been smashed to pieces over the years. But, if there were no certainties, there were plenty of fancies.

When Hatch had led his flotilla out of Singapore harbour in early March he had high hopes of the "Big One". He had been salvaging on the Admiral Stellingwerf Reef for years, mainly bringing up tin. Then

"As silent as a painted ship upon a painted ocean." The spot, miles from land, where the wreck was found, with Max's yacht in view (preceding pages).

Hatch and Max (on right) *speed over for a dive.*

Ready to go. Hatch on the lift and about to submerge.

he had found the junk, which had yielded Chinese seventeenth-century
Ming porcelain which sold at Christie's Amsterdam auction house for
almost two million pounds. This time, thanks to the decision to join
him of Max de Rham, with his years of experience – as well as his
sophisticated detection equipment – Hatch was confident that they
would sweep the Reef, and the adjacent ocean, clean.

It was a triumph of optimism over experience. Since finding the Chinese junk Hatch had twice returned to the Reef in the two brief ten-week salvaging seasons of late spring and early autumn in 1984. He had found nothing of any value. Other salvaging rivals, also aware of a possible valuable wreck in the area, had gone over the same stretch of sea. It was the use of the side-scan sonar and the magnetometer, married to the patience of Max, that forced the sea bed finally to yield up its secret.

The two men had jointly planned the expedition and jointly financed it. Their responsibilities were clear. The survey of the area and the detection of the wreck were Max de Rham's responsibility. Then Mike

The divers were lowered from the barge (left).

Hatch on the way up from the sea bed.

Hatcher took over the diving and the recovery of any valuables. They made a good team. Both were in their mid-forties and had lived in Singapore for years, building up their reputations in different but complementary fields – Max knew all about marine surveying, Hatch all about salvaging. They had worked off and on with each other in the mid-1970s.

*Working on the ocean floor.
Lines were laid down to guide
divers in the murky conditions
(right).*

*Fish were friendly companions.
They were also a good sign that
there was a wreck on the
bottom (following pages).*

And, just as their professions dovetailed, so did their characters. Mike Hatcher, born in poverty in England, sent to an orphanage at two and to Australia at thirteen, had battled his way in the world and eventually made his million through guts and hard work. He was as restless as the name of his boat, a doer rather than a thinker, an archetypal man of action. Max de Rham, born into a wealthy family in Switzerland, was a university graduate who fell in love with the sea. He had started a company specializing in marine surveying but had sold out to indulge his passion for sailing and adventure. Mike is medium height and sturdy, and Max is well over six foot and very sturdy.

So, slipping out of Singapore at the dead of night at the start of his expedition, Hatch commanded an impressive fleet – the *Restless M*, eighty feet in length, a bit battle-scarred but now full of the most modern equipment; a barge, the *Costay Nile* (soon dubbed by the team *"Costly Nile"* because of the trouble it gave them), which could moor on top of the shallow waters which just covered the Reef; and the yacht *Musichana*, with Nick Bond on board. He had helped Hatch out on other ventures and would act as a support vessel and messenger service. Max de Rham and his yacht *Star Ferry* would rendezvous with them at the Reef the next evening.

After almost twenty hours' sailing the ships reached the Reef. It is in international waters but irritatingly close to Bintan, an island that is now part of Indonesia. It gets its name from a Dutch ship which had hit the Reef in the nineteenth century, but its roll call of victims stretches up to modern times: in the early 1970's a two hundred thousand ton bulk carrier loaded with iron ore had come to grief there. The dangerous section is not much more than two hundred yards long where, at both ends, the Reef rises almost to the surface. You can stand on the two pinnacles, gazing out to sea as far as your eyes can travel before a wave knocks you off. It is these peaks, some five feet below the surface, which have claimed the lives of so many vessels and so many men.

Hatch's expedition was almost over before it began. On the first night that the party anchored together at the Reef there was a most tremendous storm. The big rubber dinghy on the barge was washed overboard and lost, and the kitchen area of the *Costly Nile* was swamped. It was an ominous start.

The first days' work went little better. As an overture, Hatch decided to do what he had done on many previous occasions: examine the surface of the Reef for tin. Using a stinger, a water jet that blasts away the coral, the divers had some frustrating days. Local fishermen, in their desire for easy pickings, had been dynamiting the Reef: it is a quick way of gathering fish but it had killed and compacted the coral, and little tin was recovered.

While the divers were thus engaged, Max de Rham and Biji assisted by Nick Bond set about surveying the Reef. The first task was to erect a prefabricated metal tower on the Reef which could be used as the centre of reference for the survey. What with currents and winds it is very easy to cover the same stretch of water continually in the middle of the ocean in the absence of a fixed point. It was a strange sight, this tower, its base eighteen feet below the surface of the Reef, its mast sticking up over a flat and featureless expanse of water. The Reef was too shallow to bring into play the side-scan sonar, and in any case any interesting finds would lie hidden beneath the coral, outside its reach, but the magnetometer was towed behind *Star Ferry*, searching for ferrous or ferromagnetic objects.

With one of the divers, usually Hans or Dorian, directing the progress of the ship from the top of the tower by theodolite and two-way radio, the magnetometer traced over the surface of the Reef along lines thirty feet apart: at this distance even the smallest objects should be detected. At the same time, every fifty metres, the depth of the water was plotted. Within five days Max could offer Hatch a complete magnetic survey of the Reef as well as a plan of its shape and depth. Often, the magnetometer indicated something on the sea bed and a diver would go down to check it out. Often, it turned out to be a can of tar: one of the vessels to hit the Reef in recent years had been carrying thousands of cans of tar. There was one large magnetic anomaly which did look intriguing, but unfortunately it was well covered by coral.

There was only one way to clear away the coral and enable a diver to investigate. The *Costly Nile* was moved over the spot and the stinger, powered by an engine on the barge, blasted its way through five feet of dead coral. There was definitely something underneath. Max dived down and quickly discovered a huge anchor. Recovering it was another matter. It was much too heavy to lift it manually but "Big Zack", following Max down, managed to attach a wire sling, and the anchor was winched out. They then recovered a second anchor which weighed an incredible three tons and measured twenty feet long by fifteen feet wide.

The first anchor was returned to the sea bed to act as a marker and, in high excitement, the divers set about combing the area. Surely a massive wreck must be close by. They found nothing. They had to make some decisions. The anchors suggested a ship somewhere in the neighbourhood. Perhaps it had drifted off the Reef. If so, given the prevailing winds, it would have gone to the south. They were sufficiently encouraged to authorize a detailed survey of the south of the Reef, up to four nautical miles. The sea bed was never more than one hundred and fifty feet below the surface, making it just within the scope of the divers. But, with little guarantee of success, while half the team plunged the deep water the other half would try and extract yet more tin from the Reef.

Working under water is very exhausting, especially when lifting heavy objects.

So the same dreary process started up again. Hans and Dorian took it in turns to mount the Reef-top tower to direct operations and, this time, because they were probing deeper water, the *Restless M* became the master vessel, purring very, very slowly up and down at one hundred metre intervals, trailing behind it the side-scan sonar "fish" and the magnetometer, as well as the marker buoy. Electronic pulses shoot down the towing cable to the "fish" which converts them to sonar pulses. The regular clicks provide a print-out on the monitoring paper, constantly being examined by Max or Biji in the tiny cabin. If a stronger echo is sent back, the colouring on the roll of paper goes darker and they know that there might be something of interest on the sea bed. With his experience Max could usually tell by the shape of any image whether it was worth dropping the marker buoy and sending down a diver.

What made the work particularly exhausting was the presence in the sea of intrusive ferromagnetic volcanic rocks, which showed up boldly on both the side-scan sonar and the magnetometer. Some of them were also confusingly shaped like wrecks. Each had to be investigated. On one occasion the German diver Hans, going down to check out a good reading, was sure that a particular outcrop was the protruding wooden remains of the buried hull of a ship. Only by hammering at the rock was he convinced of his error. Taken with the strong currents, the poor visability on the sea bed, and the known presence of sharks in the area, it was hardly surprising that morale slumped. Each evening Max and Biji poured over the reams and reams of magnetometer and side-scan sonar paper, checking once again for any conceivable sign.

So it was a boring time. The weather was hot; the sea a deep blue, except for the area around the Reef where it showed up dark green. The working day started at sun-rise and ended at sun-set, always the same time at this spot almost on the Equator. The only relief from the monotonous processing were the trips on the dinghy to the *Costay Nile* for meals. The barge was also used for sleeping accommodation, in a portacabin which slept twelve in bunks. There were few pleasures, although it was a relief to splash around in cold fresh water on the barge, with the occasional hot shower on the *Restless M*. Everyone was rationed to just one beer a day, handed out after dinner, which was usually fish. Hatch maintained firm discipline.

And so it went on for weeks. Every evening, before an early bed at nine or ten, Mike would cheer on his twelve-man team, for in addition

to the divers there were sailors and a chef on board, as well as photographer John Bremmer, brought along to record the trip. But the costs were denting even Hatch's enthusiasm – food, brought in constantly from Singapore, fuel for the engines, the cost of hiring the equipment at daily rates, all were pushing up the expenses. In addition there was the waste of time: while Hatch was out on his adventure he was missing out on valuable salvaging commissions from oil companies or marine insurance firms. The crew were on "no cure – no pay" terms, which meant that, apart from food and accommodation, they received nothing in wages but a generous percentage of anything found by the expedition. For them it looked like a wasted journey. They started to get light-headed, spending more time hunting fish underwater and taking out the surf-boards. To keep failure from his mind Hatch played endless games of backgammon with Max.

Hatch very deliberately chooses as divers men who have an easy-going temperament, who fit in well. They are invariably settled and married, not foot-loose young hot-heads. But even this experienced, industrious team got fed up with days of unproductive trawling of the same small stretch of water; with fish, fish, and yet more fish for food; and with evenings around a cassette player, listening to the same old stories, or watching videos on board the *Restless M.*

Hatch had done his best to keep up morale by varying the work. The barge was moved to where the Chinese junk had been found in 1983 and a few shards and the very occasional complete porcelain piece were found by the divers. But by early May, Hatch had decided to call off the whole enterprise. It was Max who persuaded him to keep going for two more days. And then it happened. A large object appeared on the side-scan sonar. The marking of the spot; the dive; and the discoveries. At the last moment, Hatch and the team were in business.

For most of the next six weeks, until the weather started to close in, diving conditions were excellent, and the wreck was clearly visible to the divers. Very little of the ship remained, only about three metres of the hull, but it could be measured easily and came out at thirty-six metres long and around ten metres wide. It was a big vessel, and the size of the anchor and of the cannon – found at all angles, some lying on the sand, some sticking upright – suggested that it was an important one. Quickly the *Costay Nile* was brought to cover the spot, and a line tied down to the anchor. Hatch gave the crew a lecture on security: there were to be no letters home. Already his operations on the Reef had attracted gangs of Australian rivals.

The wives were told not to expect their men back for some time and the exuberant team set about salvaging their belated discovery.

Max's sketch-map of the wreck, with the cannons marked. The guns were used by the divers to find their bearings on the sea bed. The gold was discovered outside the galley on the right.

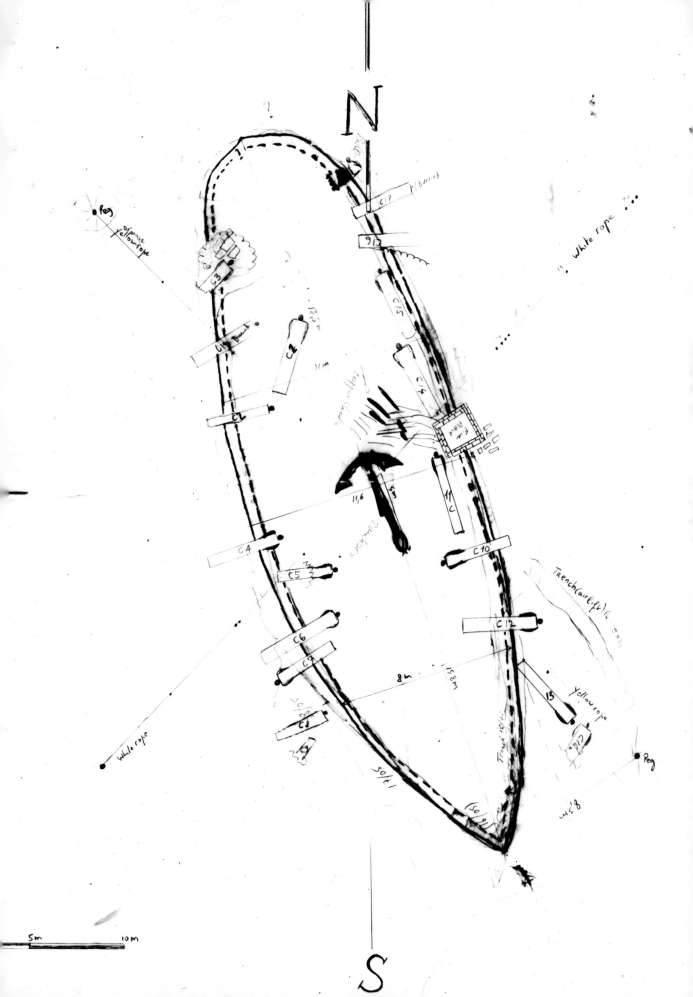

A sight for tired eyes – tea bowls and saucers by the thousand.

Fish were everywhere, even around the gold (following pages).

Although archaeological data was not uppermost in Hatch's mind, he set about the investigation of the vessel with some method. First, it was delineated and measured, a trench five feet deep being dug round it with the help of the airlift, a machine like a vast vacuum cleaner which sucked out the sand and the accumulated debris of the sea bed.

The airlift was not without its problems. It gave one diver a nasty fright when it became clogged with matter, which cut off the gushing water which acts as the driving force, filling the vacuum with air and forcing the airlift to the surface with the diver holding on for dear life. But in the main the airlift and the stinger were the most useful tools for the underwater labourers. Within a few days what was left of the wreck was revealed. Much of the wood which had not disappeared completely was riddled with the calcium left by worms, and it was impossible to tell the bow from the stern. But, in the first stroke of luck to help Hatch, the vessel had sunk upright. It was a perfect wreck to excavate.

With the ship delineated, the next task was to provide some markers for the divers. Conditions on the sea bed can vary greatly, not only in terms of visibility but also in the actual geography of the place. A change in the currents can transform the lie of the land, and it could take many minutes of precious time for a diver to re-locate himself on each descent. The cannons, however, proved useful markers and they were each individually tagged. They were the essential signposts for the salvage. But before anything could be recovered another trench had to be dug, this time round the hull, the most likely spot for profitable finds.

As the divers, wearing full gear in these cool and dangerous depths, close to the limit of practical easy salvaging, set about their preparations, they could not avoid seeing that they had had struck it rich. There were plates, bowls, tea pots, mugs in profusion, all packed tight with sand and debris. Hatch quickly realized that he needed more equipment, more divers, another barge. He returned to Singapore, taking with him some of the porcelain. James Spencer, a Christie's Chinese ceramics expert, was summoned to identify the finds. He immediately recognized them as eighteenth-century porcelain.

So, as he returned to his find, Hatch was in high spirits. He was towing another, large barge, the fifty-metre-square *Engineer*, which had on board a large crane, an air compressor, a gantry, two more portacabins, and four divers. There was also a tug with a six-man crew to add muscle. The *Engineer* was placed over the site of the wreck and lashed to the *Costay Nile*. Even in the roughest weather the barges would remain stable. Had Hatch attempted to lift the porcelain on to the *Restless M*, much of it would have smashed as it hit the heaving

One of the large plates which raised the divers' spirits.

decks. It was the barges that were to receive the precious finds.

But before all this costly equipment could be put to work, disaster struck. A sudden storm came out of Sumatra, breaking the bonds that linked the rafts, and throwing the machinery around. It became obvious that the operation could only be effectively mounted if the equipment was put into place in calm waters, and so Hatch slowly hauled his flotilla away to where the damage could be repaired and everything fitted out for what he hoped would be the final assault on the wreck. Marker buoys were dropped to signal its position.

The repairs were completed and the ships set out again to sea. Soon they were at the Reef, but where were the marker buoys? They had completely disappeared. Hatch seemed to have lost his wreck.

He cursed the local fishermen – he supposed that they had stolen the worthless buoys – and set about with Max going through all the recordings taken from the Reef-top tower. Whenever anything interesting had shown up on the sonar the bearing had been marked.

Treasures of the deep.

A cannon is hauled onto the barge – another clue towards the identification of the wreck.

There was nothing else to it but to investigate again the spots dived earlier, and, thanks to Max's meticulous records, this proved easy.

After the setbacks of the storm and the disappearing buoys, Hatch's luck was about to turn. As the *Restless M* arrived at the most hopeful reading from the past records, Hatch noticed a buoy bobbing around just below the surface. The storm's currents had dragged it under. Finally everything was ready again and the serious salvaging could begin. Already too many days had been wasted – and the storms had started. On May 28, 1985, almost three weeks after the wreck had first revealed itself on the sonar, the divers plunged into the deep.

A routine was quickly established. Hatch had ten divers at his disposal, including himself and Max. They always dived in pairs and invariably in the same pairs. It can be very dangerous on the sea bed, the main problem being the entangling of the lines supplying the oxygen. You need a good friend and a familiar worker alongside you. A rhythm, a method, is created. Invariably your partner below the surface is your best friend on deck. You rely on each other.

The pairs dived twice a day, the first shift starting at seven in the morning and operations ending at six-thirty, just before sun-set. The

Pots by the bucket-load.

The barge gave stability (right)
– it hardly moved even in the
roughest seas.

first dive would last fifty minutes, the second less than forty. After
every dive it was straight into the decompression chamber where a
tedious half hour was spent adjusting to the differences in pressure
under water and on the surface. On one or two occasions divers showed
signs of getting the bends, the feared cramps caused by the nitrogen

absorbed while under water being released from the body too rapidly. The bends can kill, but by throwing the divers quickly back into the water, putting them under the same pressure, and then bringing them to the surface slowly, the attacks can be overcome. Hatch prides himself on never having lost a diver, dead: there have been a few hospital cases.

During the whole expedition there was only one nasty moment. Dorian woke up one night with a pain in his arm: it could have been a nitrogen bubble. Anxious not to wake the rest of the tired crew, he attempted to put on his diving gear. He planned to go underwater and come out again more slowly – the old-fashioned way to beat the bends.

Fortunately Hash, the chief diver, heard him and promptly pushed him into the decompression chamber where he had to stay for many hours.

Working on the sea bed, with a pressure of around one hundred and thirty feet of water on top of you, is about five times harder than working on the surface. The bottom pressure is about sixty pounds a square inch, which forces nitrogen into your blood. Due to the pressure to work quickly on the wreck, the dangers of nitrogen poisoning were very real. But the safety precautions were precise. Every diver was controlled from above, with his air supplied from the surface. On arrival at the sea bed, the diver's hose was clipped to the lift and he was allowed a forty-five foot working radius. His controller on the surface would tell him when his time was up and then he just followed his hose to the lift, and told surface to haul him up. Then off with the gear and into the decompression chamber.

From the start Hatch and his team were amazed at the enormity of their find. The first loose pieces of porcelain that they discovered came from chests that had been smashed open by the falling cannon. But

After the diving, there was the cleaning. Breakages were kept to a minimum.

Gold – Hatch holds a fortune.

Some sea bed encrustation was allowed to remain on the finds.

most of the chests were firmly intact. Indeed they had to be prised open. The first revealed tea bowls and saucers packed very tightly in some brown glutinous substance. It did not take long for the divers to realize that this was, appropriately enough, tea. As they later learned, tea was the most valuable commodity, and the eighteenth-century merchants had thrown in the porcelain, not as ballast exactly, but very much as run-of-the-mill back-up.

The chests were packed tightly up against each other in what turned out to be the bow of the wreck. Crate after crate contained tea bowls and saucers. In fact the divers became fed up with unloading such a monotonous cargo. But their spirits rose when they discovered a chest full of beer mugs: here was something they could identify with. Then they realized that packed inside the mugs were yet more bowls and saucers.

For the divers much of the salvaging was arduous and boring. There was the cumbersome and lengthy business of dressing each other in full professional divers' gear. Then each would step on to a stage which would be slowly lowered into the water. Within a minute or so they would be jumping out on to their temporary work surface. Some days they toiled under the glare of arc lights; occasionally the weather was so bad they could not work at all.

Their main tool was the airlift, which blew away the sand and coral and marine detritus and exposed the crates and the loose porcelain. One diver would operate this while the other would carry the porcelain by the armful to the lift, a one-metre-square steel box, which was lowered after the divers and which held six plastic rubbish baskets, with drainage holes. The finds were placed in these buckets and when they were full the signal was given to the surface to haul up the box. To try and liven up this exhausting work the divers competed to see which pair could pack up the most porcelain in one fifty-minute stint. The record was twelve baskets full of dinner plates, seven hundred pieces in all.

There was no break during the long days. As soon as one pair of divers surfaced another pair took their place down under. The quantity of porcelain to salvage was outside anyone's imagination. It was far and away the biggest find of its kind, well exceeding the amount of eighteenth-century Chinese porcelain that would be offered to the market through the world's auction houses over many years. But worries about its saleability were the least of Hatch's concerns. He knew he had a limited time before the weather crowded in. His main task was transporting what had been found to Singapore, although he took every opportunity to dive too.

The miracle was that the cargo had remained virtually intact. This was thanks to the tea as much as to the slow sinking of the vessel. The tea held the porcelain firm in its glutinous grip. But if it ensured its survival, it also made conditions very hard for the divers. It rose up from the chests clouding their visibility; its thick clogging smell made breathing difficult. It was everywhere, a dark, pungent slime. It was like searching in a tea pot, especially when the weather was stormy and currents whirled around the divers.

But at least no time had to be wasted on the sea bed searching for the porcelain: it stretched all around them. Sometimes, when the airlift had pumped away all the debris, they discovered a chest that had been hit by a falling cannon, breaking every single plate or bowl with an identical crack. All the shards were ignored as were most slightly broken objects. There were more than enough in perfect condition. So up they came, the tea bowls and saucers, the soup plates and butter tubs, the jugs and tureens, virtually all made of blue and white porcelain and covered with the familiar Chinese scenes, of fishermen and pagodas, pine trees and peonies. It became tedious as well as exhausting.

Yet whenever concentration flagged a new discovery would lift the spirits. As they moved down the ship, divers Samsi and Zainal came across a chest which was found to contain enormous fish dishes, large blue and white deep dishes, forty-five centimetres in diameter and decorated with exotic carp surrounded by flowers. Over thirty of these were carefully brought to the surface.

After the hull had yielded up its cargo of mainly tea bowls and saucers another trench was dug down from the stern to the centre of the wreck. The divers were anxious to get to the cabin area. They were rewarded with the discovery of much better quality porcelain, the private goods of the officers, which in the eighteenth century could be expected to fetch high prices through individual sales, as well as some presents for loved ones. Here were found figures of Immortals and ladies, an intriguing seated boy and a glazed parrot, and much more.

By this time they were working hurriedly, hardly examining the chocolate cups and queer-shaped bowls which were later to divide the experts — were they chamber pots for children or vomit cups? As the weather deteriorated so did the working conditions. Sometimes the divers could hardly move for the discarded material which was crowding the space and shifting with the currents. As the porcelain was loaded into the buckets on the box, tens, and tens, and tens, of thousands of pieces, the divers began to think they had done enough. There were also disappointments: a crate could be laboriously opened to be full only of congealed tea.

By June 22, Hatch, too, was talking about leaving. There were more and more days on which diving was impossible and the wreck seemed

Immortals – private cargo goods, belonging to the officers and destined for the Dutch burghers.

Job lots: the divers' pay depended on the outcome of the auction so everything was carefully handled (preceding page and left).

to have yielded up all its excessive bounty, once the divers had turned over the cabin area. Early on, they had learned to be very careful as they washed the porcelain on the barge. Out of mugs and jars could tumble jewels and small statues and glasses. It was agreed that nothing should be held back: everything was to be auctioned. If a diver was fond of a particular object he had found, he could bid for it later. Only the cracked pieces could be retained. In the event most of the divers now have small, but select, collections from the wreck.

While Hatch arranged the departure from the site, it was agreed that there should be a meticulous exploration of the area outside the hull. A trench was dug on the off-chance that objects might have fallen over the sides of the ship during its death throes. Soon the collapsed cookhouse, the brick wall which Hatch and Max had found on that first exploratory dive over a month previously, was reached. Hatch was getting out of the decompression chamber; Max was getting ready to dive. It was Dorian who was sucking away at the bricks with his airlift on the sea bed. Suddenly he gasped through his speaking tube, "Surface! Surface!" Both Max and Hatch thought he was in trouble. Then the magic words which were to transform Hatch's expedition into the stuff of dreams – "Gold. I found gold."

Dorian had come across a copper-coloured object, eight centimetres wide, two-and-a-half centimetres deep and one-and-a-half centimetres high. As he picked it up, he realized by its weight that it was not what it seemed. He rubbed at the surface and there it was – gold. Pandemonium broke loose on the surface, with all the divers shouting down at him through the intercom. "How heavy?", "How much?", "What shape?". It was chaotic until Hatch yelled: "Silence." And there was silence until twenty minutes later Dorian staggered on to the deck.

Dorian had stuffed as many of the bars as he could find into his diving suit. As he unzipped it, they fell out before his excited mates, seventeen small ingots in all. There was great cheering, but for Dorian it was off with his clothes and straight into the decompression chamber.

Immediately there was a rush to dive the spot. Max was next down. He was working in complete darkness but he knew he was handling gold as soon as he touched a bar, its gleam beckoning to him through the murky depths. Then all the divers had a turn, with keen competition to find the most bars. Appropriately enough it was Hatch who came up with the most, twenty-nine bars out of a final total of one hundred and twenty-five.

The gold was the perfect icing on the cake. It proved to be Chinese gold of an hitherto unknown shape, and individual ingots were eventually to sell for over £50,000, well in excess of their bullion value of nearer £2,000. The romance of its discovery, and its unique shape, made it desirable to collectors.

While marketing of the porcelain would be enough to make Hatch his second – or, with the money he had got from salvaging tin, his third – fortune, coming across the gold would ensure that the discovery of the wreck would fire the imagination of the man in the street rather than just the collector of Chinese works of art. It would make Hatch famous.

The next six days were an anticlimax. Little of any value was found and diving conditions were becoming treacherous. But the gold kept the spirits high. It also seemed to make an identification of the wreck that much easier. There was no conclusive evidence yet and Hatch was still maintaining absolute secrecy about his find, but already most of the pieces in the jigsaw had fitted into place.

It had been a very successful expedition which would pay for its cost many times over. There had been problems – the long search for the wreck after the quick discovery of the anchors; the sudden storms, which had forced repairs on the barges; the temporary loss of the marker buoys. There had also been a nasty moment when the propellor of the tug had caught the *Costay Nile*'s anchor cable and could only be detached by sacrificing the anchor to the sea bed. (In a way it was a nice memento: something from Hatch to excite, and disappoint, some future salavager around the Reef.) Perhaps most gratifying of all, there had been no casualties – just three temporary cases of the bends – and less than two per cent of the porcelain discovered intact had been broken during the recovery operation.

This says much for the part Nick Bond played in cleaning and packing the porcelain. All the divers mucked in in washing off the marine detritus but Nick was in charge of the unglamorous, laborious, but absolutely essential job of ensuring that it reached Singapore in one piece – or rather in over 160,000 pieces.

Hatch had picked his team well. Apart from Max, whose expertise had located the wreck, there was Dorian, an Englishman who had come late to professional diving and who was on his first expedition with Hatch; there was Hans, an experienced German, who had worked the oil rigs; there was chief diver Hash, who found the first crate of porcelain, and the other, mainly Malay, divers with their inexhaustible passion for hunting fish – a poor return, since the fish had welcomed the divers to their home, and had become familiar allies.

Max, in particular, made friends with a large grouper which followed him around on his sea bed tasks. They became great buddies, Max tickling the grouper's belly and the grouper swimming up close while he worked. It was a sad evening when one of the Malay divers came to the surface with a dead fish which was obviously Max's own grouper. There were tough men who could not eat their dinner, fish, that night.

Other fish were less welcoming. Mory eels and sting rays can kill but only if they feel threatened, and they are as anxious to avoid humans as

The daily round – two dives each and then on to washing the finds.

humans are to avoid them. Of sharks there were few signs, although divers take a fairly easy going attitude to the creatures. In these waters they feed well and rarely attack humans. The only sour note in this happy relationship between diver and diver (and between diver and fish) was the behaviour of the crew on the tug. Soon after his fleet arrived back in Singapore, porcelain bowls and dishes, obviously from the wreck, started to be offered at a local antique shop: over a hundred items were found to be missing and Hatch points the finger at his casual labour.

This was not quite the end of the expedition to hunt the Admiral Stellingwerf Reef. While a container ship steamed slowly to Europe with its cargo of 1,400 large cartons packed with porcelain from the wreck, which would take six people more than a month to unpack, clean and store, Dr Jorg, a historian at Groningen University, came up with the original inventory of a Dutch East Indiaman. It was called the *Geldermalsen*. But if it was this ship which had sunk in the area there should have been more gold on the sea bed, and, in all, 240,000 pieces of porcelain, as against the 170,000 that Hatch's team had recovered.

More to the point, if the wreck could be conclusively proved to be the *Geldermalsen*, the planned sale would go that much better: it really would be the identifiable past come to life again. Christie's, the auctioneers chosen by Hatch to organize the sale, were becoming racked with doubt as to whether there could possibly be enough buyers for such a vast, such an unprecedented quantity of Chinese porcelain. It had already given the find a name, the "Nanking Cargo," an expert's in-joke: in the eighteenth century such a cargo of porcelain would be advertized in European cities as coming from Nanking, even though specialists now know it was made further inland in China. Also Nanking had a reassuring oriental sound without being too specific about the actual origin of the porcelain.

There was also the position of the Dutch Government to be considered. It was convinced that Hatch had discovered the *Geldermal-sen*. If he had, there was a good legal case that anything salvaged belonged to the Netherlands as the natural successor to the Dutch East India Company. Hatch met with all the Dutch legal, historical and political top-brass and came to a deal. He would go back to the site and attempt to furnish irrefutable proof: in exchange, proceeds from any sale would be split, with the Dutch Government getting ten per cent. To begin with it had wanted twenty-five per cent, but since Hatch had the better hand he had his way. By making this agreement he, for the first time, had some legal right to the wreck: the whole position of who owns ships lost at sea is confused and contentious.

So early in March 1986, while arrangements were far advanced for a five-day auction in Amsterdam in late April, Hatch set to sea again with the *Restless M* and his team. There was no difficulty in re-locating the site, and diving started once more. But this time the laws of chance seemed to be in operation; Hatch was not to be so lucky again. Only one gold bar was found, but inside the hull another chest was discovered. It contained yet more tea bowls and saucers. Three soup plates were recovered, and other odds and ends. That was all.

Then there was the find which meant little in immediate financial return but everything to the ultimate success of the auction at Christie's. The ship's bell had been located and hauled to the surface. Its Latin inscription offered another vital clue. It did not name the ship but it gave its date and when it was cast: 1747, the year in which the *Geldermalsen* was completed. Two large bronze cannon were brought up, one cast in Rotterdam and one in Amsterdam which at least confirmed the nationality as Dutch. Finally there was the clinching clue: a surgeon's seal with the initials F.B., recovered from a cabin which also contained broken medicine bottles: the surgeon on the *Geldermalsen* was Frederik Berkenhouwer.

With these later finds, no-one now doubted the identity of the ship. Hatch had located the last resting place of the *Geldermalsen* .

But there was little time for a requiem. A week after they had arrived at the old hunting ground they were visited by an Indonesian naval vessel which politely asked them what they were up to. They protested that they were in international waters but the Indonesians had the bigger guns. They were allowed three days to pack up and so, with the bell, the two large bronze cannon, one hundred and sixty boxes of porcelain and one gold bar they departed for Singapore.

It is possible that Hatch will one day return to the wreck but whether he does or not, other hopeful salvagers will search it out. The Indonesians have certainly been back, in August 1986, and with tragic results – a young marine archaeologist was lost while diving the wreck. It has many attractions – to archaeologists, who are as much interested in its timbers and its shape as in its cargo, and to treasure hunters, who know that over twenty gold bars are missing from the original manifest of the ship. It seems unlikely that the survivors of the wreck in their ordeal, would have had the time, or the will, to hide away the gold. Somewhere near the Reef could be gold to the value of at least £500,000, and perhaps more chests of porcelain.

Hatch thinks that the Admiral Stellingwerf Reef has now been dived dry, although his own record of fruitless searches and then unexpected prizes suggests that he could be wrong. But anyone going out there has to chance their arm with a suspicious Indonesian Government, and be experienced and well equipped. It was the high precision equipment that Max de Rham brought to the enterprise which ensured its success.

For Hatch, it has proved the start of another career at the peak point of his life. He was forty-five when he found the *Geldermalsen*, a stocky, balding man, obviously incredibly fit and with a tough, uncompromising, attitude to life. He has bright blue eyes, a direct manner, a hatred of authority and cities, and an insatiable need for a challenge. He has now given up salvaging modern vessels. He is away at sea looking for more wrecks from past centuries. Rich and famous, hard yet somehow innocent, he has created a remarkable personality, and history, from very unpromising beginnings.

2

Salvaging a Fortune

From the start Mike Hatcher's life was the stuff of drama, bordering on tragedy. He was born in York, not in the elegant centre of this ancient northern English city but in a working-class suburb. His father, a bricklayer, was soon off defending the country, for these were the early days of the Second World War. Both his parents found romantic consolations amid the turmoil, and Mike and his younger sister Jess were sufficiently neglected for worried neighbours to call the welfare service to the house. His mother had no objection to her children being taken into care. Parental rejection when he was barely two must have helped to sow the seeds of the independence that Mike Hatcher has exhibited all his life.

The children were sent away to Dr Barnardo's orphanage and spent a spartan but not unhappy childhood at homes in Tunbridge Wells in Kent. Only in recent years has Mike been able to tie together his family history. With fame and fortune, half-brothers and half-sisters, parents as well, have appeared from the shadows. He now has a rueful acceptance of his father who has spent a careless life marrying (sometimes when he still had a legal wife) and spawning children, while creating, and just as quickly losing, fortunes as a building contractor. Father George jumped ship in Australia after the War and did well for a time from the property boom. He still lives there.

If his father contributed adventurous blood and itchy feet to Hatch, his taste for danger comes from his grandfather, Arthur, who received an award for gallantry in 1922 when working down a pit in Barnsley — he threw himself in front of a runaway truck in order to protect his comrades, losing his sight and the use of his legs for his effort.

When he was thirteen Hatch unknowingly followed his father to Australia, which in those days was keen to welcome British immigrants, especially young boys wide-eyed at the idea of working as cowboys in the Outback. Dr Barnardo's, trying to cope with the surplus of children thrown into its care by the War, was equally glad to pass them on to farm schools there. Hatch has a warm spot for Dr Barnardo's (he has donated generously to it from his fortune) but he thinks the institution was preying on the innocence of boys in sending

Hatch as Dr Barnardo's knew him.

them around the world to an uncertain future. Hatch has equally mixed feelings about Australia. Its open ways enabled him to make his first million. It has also given him an accent. But he has had constant battles with the authorities there and still retains British citizenship.

The battles began on his first day at farm school. His "pommie" accent was quickly mocked and just as quickly a fight followed. Hatch held the record for the number of canings in one day at school in England – over twenty – and he was not going to be pushed around. Similar tussles followed, as Hatch was sent off to a farm after learning the rudiments of agriculture. He skipped his first job after a day because the farmer's wife refused to let him wash off in a bath the filth he'd brought in from the cowsheds. His second posting was to a dubious bachelor who expected the fifteen-year-old boy to share his bed. It was only on his sixth farm that Hatch hit lucky with a family of Plymouth Bretheren who treated him decently.

But the next few years were the dreariest of his life. In the end the steady mechanization of farm work saved him. He became fascinated by machinery and started to study engineering at night school. By his early twenties he had escaped to Sydney, where he worked on the installation of swimming pools. The good life was just round the corner.

He was earning reasonable money by now, had joined the local surf club, involved himself in scuba diving, was crewing in yacht races, leading, in fact, the typical outdoor life of a young Australian male. He was also meeting girls. It was a girl who opened the door to his future.

Hatch (on the right) *as he set off round the world on* Islander III.

Her father made Bar-B-Que sets in New Zealand. Mike thought they would sell well in prospering Australia and was given the task of proving his theory. In the mornings he knocked on doors selling, in the afternoons he was delivering the Bar-B-Ques. By the age of twenty-seven he no longer had a girlfriend but he had made enough money to buy his first boat.

With no ties, a little cash, an aversion already to paying tax, and some casual companions, Hatcher decided to sail round the world in his boat, *Islander III*. He took a long time to get a very little way. A year later, minus his companions, he had reached New Guinea. There he scraped a living in the time-honoured way by selling trade goods – tobacco, cloth

– to the tribesmen in return for their wood carvings. On the day he reached Bourgainville he had just fifty cents left in his pocket. He naturally went straight to the local yacht club – a tin shack with an aimiable bar manager – to buy a beer. He asked what were the prospects for a flat-broke sailor in that remote spot. They were surprisingly bright: by hiring out his yacht by the day to the well-paid miners in the local copper mine, and also by selling them the native carvings, Hatcher was soon back in funds.

It was an idyllic life. And it was here that Hatcher first dived for money. While chartering his boat out along the coast, he had come across a group of divers hacking copper and any other saleable metal from the remains of a sunken Second World War destroyer. Hatcher got friendly with them and started to dive for fun. He liked it enough to ask for a job. He had, in this casual way, begun his career as a professional diver and salvager.

At night the divers would sit around discussing the great wrecks which had gone down with prize cargoes – the ships scuppered at the fall of Singapore or downed by submarines; the older, treasure-laden, Dutch East Indiamen; even further back in history, the Chinese junks trading between the Chinese mainlaind and the islands of what is now Indonesia, many of which had come to grief in the treacherous waters of the South China Sea. For these men, and for Hatcher, the talk was just dreams. To salvage such wrecks you need a boat, costly equipment and plenty of time, a capital investment way beyond the hopes of jobbing divers getting by hacking metal off sunken Second World War freighters.

Soon being one of a team palled for Hatcher. He had had enough by now and wanted to dive on his own account. He also wanted to try for the big prizes. He sailed *Islander III* west along the New Guinea coast towards Indonesia, single-handed once more but this time cushioned by a few thousand dollars. But he was not quite experienced enough to start his own company. While waiting for an Indonesian visa he fell in with an old beachcomber who just happened to own the salvaging rights in a bay which contained more than its fair share of wrecks. This man loaned Hatcher a barge and told him to get on with it.

For four months Hatcher worked the bay, bringing up copper pipes, perhaps the odd propeller or rusting anchor, which he sold to the beachcomber. It was a living but not a challenge. The challenge lay in Singapore. So, quitting New Guinea and the lotus-eating life of the drifters, Hatcher headed west once more.

Singapore was not the great salvaging metropolis that the fancies of the New Guinea divers had conjured up. There were just three companies prospecting for wrecks and bringing up scrap and cargo. The new boy did not think he had much to learn about salvaging – but he soon discovered that he was a total innocent at business.

Hatcher decided to make Singapore his base. He sold his boat and fell in with a group of experienced salvagers. There was talk of a wreck along the Malaysian coast which had been given a light going-over but the amateurish raiders were not thought to have touched its hold. Blowing open a hold to get at the cargo requires explosives and skill: most wreck divers want the easy, quickly disposable outer pickings.

The deal was that Hatcher should go and look for the wreck while his partners handled the marketing of any worthwhile pickings. The ship did not prove an elusive quarry: it was aground on a beach and partly visible at low tide. The wreck had been stripped of its funnel and bridge but the hold containing tin and rubber was as sealed tight as on the day it sailed out of Singapore. Soon Hatcher was learning how to prise open a hold and bring to the surface the tin and the rubber which in the mid 1970s were in great demand and commanded very high prices. All told, that cargo produced commodities worth seven million dollars. Hatcher was down to get seventeen per cent of the take. In the event he got little above his wages of three thousand dollars a month. The rest had mysteriously disappeared in "expenses."

He was now determined to run his own business. He bought another boat, invested in better salvaging equipment, and put himself out for hire. He went anywhere, recovering from a sunken fishing boat here, a lost aeroplane there, on his own initiative or on commission from others. At this time there were still plenty of Second World War wrecks to be salvaged in the South China Seas. Any money he made went on better equipment. And his reputation grew.

But there was still the problem that he did not have the resources to be able to spend the time looking for the really lucrative wrecks. For that, he needed backers and there were now many local millionaires willing to gamble on Hatcher's expertise.

His first venture in a partnership was another failure. After five months of searching he located a prime Second World War wreck on a reef. He set to, bringing up the cargo and arranging for it to be shipped back to Singapore for disposal on the market. After an arduous six months, during which he hardly left his boat, he returned for his share of the booty – to discover a bare cupboard. His partners had splashed out on big cars and lavish offices leaving Hatch only enough money to pay off his team of divers. He was back to square one.

Using their majority shareholding, Hatch's "backers" had sold the company to a rich Chinese businessman, with the bait that Hatcher knew where there was gold. Flat-broke, Hatch went to meet the financial adviser to his new boss – and met Ong. Soo Hin Ong, a London-educated accountant, was impressed with Hatch, impressed enough to hand over a cheque for one thousand dollars to keep him going, gold or no gold. The second member of the team that was to bring up the Nanking cargo had entered the story. Ong called Hatch "the yacht club bum", but he recognized his skill in making money from the bottom of the sea. Ong started to organize Hatcher's business affairs. He still does. He is the money man of United Subsea Services, the Panama-based company, which is the commercial face of Mike Hatcher.

The third member of the eventual team had also put in a fleeting appearance by now – Max de Rham. Max, a towering forty-seven-year-old, is the son of a Swiss diplomat who trailed him around the world in his early years. He went to Lausanne University where he studied geophysics, leaving to join the oil industry, which was just then starting on its period of expansion. After a cold, uncomfortable, year messing around in the mud of the Rhine delta for a French company, Max and a colleague decided anything was better than this, even starting up their own business. With the arrogance of youth, and a small boat that they had built themselves, the two tyros wrote to everyone they could think of offering every kind of service – water studies, discovering gravel deposits, marine surveying, they would do anything.

Not surprisingly there was no response and Max was becoming despondent, arriving later and later each morning at his Lausanne office. One day his luck turned. The young men were given an assignment to look for gravel – on a "no cure – no fee" basis, one that was to become very familiar to him. After days of disappointment the gravel miraculously revealed itself. Max was in business. The two partners promptly followed their instincts and went off sailing for a year.

Max makes a striking parallel with Mike: two men, from very different backgrounds, making their way in the world through their own initiative and then following their fancy, which in both cases was the sea. Like Hatch, Max discovered the lure of diving; like Hatch he learned his sea craft out on the waters – of the Red Sea and Med. By the time his money had run out, Max had decided that his future lay in marine engineering and surveying. He went to the US to acquaint himself with the latest technology, and was ready for business. Ironically his first major job was back in land-locked Switzerland, recovering an experimental mini-submarine which had gone down on its maiden voyage in Lake Lugano, but by the age of twenty-seven he was out in the Far East for the first time, looking after the interests of his company in that part of the world.

By 1971 Max was in New Caledonia, taking part in the nickel boom. His reputation started to travel around the area but while Max was picking up the jobs – a mine-sweeping survey here for Union Oil; some under-sea mineral searching there – his partners back in Europe were facing tougher times. They agreed to break up, and Max set up his own semi-independent operation – from a garage in Singapore.

Most of his commissions were for the oil industry, helping it in its insatiable hunt for new oil fields. Max was very much a one-man band, going off in a diving assignment, rushing back to catch up with the paper-work, before setting off again on an oceanographic operation. But he made one decision which was to determine his future – he would not buy his own boat. "We were in high technology," he says. "Boats are low technology. Also they need to be taken care of."

By ploughing all his profits back into new and better equipment Max found himself, like Mike Hatcher, with a big reputation in Singapore but not enough time, or resources, really to break into the big time. Like Hatch, once again, he needed powerful partners to finance his ambitious plans. He got together with Delauze (boss of Comex and Geomex), at the same time buying out his original partners, and, for the first time, making a great deal of money. Max soon discovered that he was spending all his energies in aircraft, flying around the world from one major job to another, with no time to indulge in his love of sailing or to enjoy his success. Finally he sold out to the expanding British company Oceanics and, after working out his contract, found himself, in 1985, financially free and with time to spare. It was natural that he should then join in with his old friend Mike Hatcher.

The two men had first met in the tough times of the mid 1970s when a recession in the oil industry had forced them to undertake any job on offer. It was Hatch with the boat, Max with his surveying skills. Their eventual partnership was forged on many messy, difficult, and often unrewarding expeditions up muddy Indonesian rivers recovering lost oil equipment. The initial meeting had not been encouraging. The meticulous Max was shocked by the scruffy look of *Seeker One*, the converted trawler which was the base of Hatch's salvaging operations. The two men had a furious row and Max went off on another boat. It hit a sandbank on the first day, and he was soon back for a conciliatory drink and for the start of a friendship which has developed into a firm business partnership.

It was the surveying knowledge of Max de Rham which eventually found the *Geldermalsen*, but in the early 1980s Max could only look on jealously, while the more liberated Hatch set about searching for wrecks. Max was still an international jet-setter, making his first million through building up a company rather than in the cut-and-thrust world of "no cure – no fee" which was to set Hatch on his way to financial independence.

From the start the Hatcher-Ong venture had prospered. Hatch may not have known where there was any gold, but he was pretty certain that he knew the rough whereabouts of a ship that had gone down smuggling tin. He managed to salvage fifteen tons of it which, at the current price of forty-thousand dollars a ton, not only gave his new partners faith in Hatch but also put their enterprise nicely into profit.

Hatch persuaded Ong that there could be even richer pickings if *Seeker One* was equipped with more sophisticated equipment. He was prepared to invest all the money he had made from the tin salvage if Ong could raise the two hundred thousand dollars required to buy sonar and radar, and to pay for Hatch to go to Norway to learn how to operate the new machinery. It proved an excellent buy.

Hatch was always on the look-out for new wrecks. An incident in a book about a British warship's adventures in the Second World War had alerted him to a German cargo boat which went down in the South China Sea carrying tin and other war materials. He had been looking for it fruitlessly for months. With the sonar he located it in two days. He sent down a grappling hook, dived, and there on the deck was tin. Five months later, with his fifty thousand dollar finder's fee from Ong and his thirty per cent from the sale of the tin, Hatch was a millionaire.

As Hatch says, "That saved my butt." From then on, he was financially secure and the offers flooded in. There were two Second World War wrecks in international waters which had been casually salvaged. There were rumours that perhaps sixty tons of tin remained below the surface. Hatch had a look – and came up with four hundred tons, and a financial return which was almost as rich as the prize from the *Geldermalsen*. "That was it. The biggest job I ever did, " he recalls.

It was the turning point in his career. Up to then he was always hasseling for other people. With the money from this assignment he hit on the formula of investing two-thirds of the take into properties and secure investments, while ploughing back the other third into better equipment for the ships. He has never sold off the land and apartments he bought in the US and Australia: they are the real treasure from his years prospecting the sea bed. He was guided in this canny approach by Ong.

While working away on these wrecks Hatch came across a Dutch submarine which had been sunk by the Japanese during the War. It brought him no financial return but led to the fourth member his eventual team – Henri Besancon.

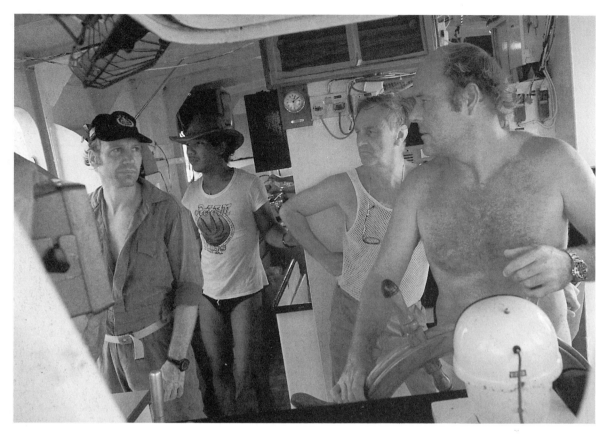

Searching for the lost Dutch submarine K-17 off the coast of Malaysia.

A diver's eye-view.

Hatch was not over-excited by the discovery of this submarine. He knew from his researches into the ships that had gone down in the area during the Second World War that two Dutch submarines had been lost on patrol. He was out doing a survey for an oil company at the time, the bread and butter work which kept the company going while the wrecks were pinpointed. But he dived down, brought up the signal lamp, which confirmed the identity of the sub, and, as a matter of form passed the information back to the naval authorities in London.

Submariners are great ones for reunions and the story quickly got back to the Netherlands that one of its submarines had been plotted. It marked the end of a quest for Henri Besancon, a Dutch naval officer and historian, who had for many years been searching for the sea bed grave of his father, the commander of this submarine. Besancon immediately contacted Hatch. He wanted to go to the site and after persuading a Dutch magazine to finance a feature on this emotional pilgrimage, Hatch agreed to take him to the spot, basically as a week-end excursion. Hatch dived for the sub's wheel which he presented to Besancon.

It was as they sailed back to Singapore that the two men got talking. Hatch complained about the shortage of modern wrecks – the accessible ones had been salvaged, and the tricky ones were not worth bothering about given the fall in the tin price. It was Besancon who turned his mind to the "oldies", to the Dutch trading vessels which had failed to make it back to the Netherlands. It was then that the *Geldermalsen* first began to infiltrate into Hatch's consciousness.

Safety for a diver depends on team-work.

Henri Besancon (centre, right) on the hunt for his father's resting place. The wheel provided some evidence.

But before that there was the *Risdam*. Besancon's researches into the area where his father's sub had been lost alerted him to the wreck of an eighteenth century Dutch ship, the *Risdam*. So, in 1983, this became the first historical find to be salvaged by Hatch. It was not a success. He brought up some artefacts including the cannon and was able to discover that the main cargo was timber, but with some choice Siamese porcelain. A *Save the Risdam* campaign got underway in the Netherlands, but before a proper excavation could be mounted the cook on Hatcher's ship had blurted out the find to a rival group in Singapore who came up, blew open the hold, and made a rough and ready attempt to seize some of the treasures.

The Malaysian authorities – the wreck is just two miles off-shore – were furious, and threw the scavengers into gaol. The whole episode taught Hatch many lessons. In future there was to be much tighter security on board his ship during an operation and, on the *Geldermalsen* dive, letters from the crew home were censored. In addition, it highlighted the need to co-operate with the authorities: only now has Hatch managed to re-build his bridges with Malaysian officials. Indeed he is confident that he will get the contract to go back and make the definite excavation of the *Risdam*, which still contains most of its cargo.

The furore over the *Risdam* was also to create problems in the Netherlands. Marine archaeologists at museums there seized on the activities of the rival gang to prove their case that historical wrecks should be left to academic experts to investigate rather than commercial salvage operators. It is the old battle between Commercial enterprise on the one hand and scholarly niceties and red tape on the other: without men like Hatch the wrecks would never be discovered, let alone recovered. But memories of the *Risdam* caused rows with the Dutch museum establishment when the Nanking cargo came to be sold by Christie's in Amsterdam two years later.

So by 1983 the team was coming together in a loose association. There was Ong, to look after the financial side, and here things were operating smoothly, thanks to the salvaged hoard of tin which allowed Hatch to indulge in the risky, costly and time-consuming hunt for old wrecks (while still undertaking salvaging commissions for oil companies or marine insurers.) There was Henri Besancon in the Netherlands, pouring over old charts, records and books in the museums and sending the leads to Singapore. And, waiting on the sidelines, there was Max de Rham, still working for Oceanics but becoming increasingly interested in wrecks, and, like Hatch, well aware of the existence of the "G." Perhaps, at this stage, Max was as much a rival as the partner he later became.

The most likely spot for wrecks was the Admiral Stellingwerf Reef, just south of Singapore, where masters of vessels from China on passage to Europe started to think about turning north to enter the Straits of Malacca. In the eighteenth century, captains stayed as close as possible to land, but this Reef, just below the surface of the water, had brought down enough modern ships to make it very familiar to Hatch. He had salvaged tin there; brought up coins; usually stopped for a speculative dive if he was passing by it.

It was Hatch who had followed up Henri Besancon's advice and checked out the evidence of the survivors of the *Geldermalsen* as it was written down in the archives in The Hague. The survivors said that they could not see land from the shoal where they claimed the ship had run aground. But, from the same spot, Hatch could distinctly make out the coastline. Obviously the "G" had sunk somewhere else, and by the look of the currents it was to the east. It might have been the notorious Admiral Stellingwerf.

In the spring of 1983, as Hatch sailed out of Singapore at the start of his hundred-mile journey, there was a strange mixture of seriousness and light-heartedness on board. For years he had undertaken difficult and dangerous assignments, on orders from others and more recently on his own account, salvaging metal for re-processing into modern machines. It was profitable work, but had lacked the tang of adventure which had taken him away from Australia almost twenty years previously. This time there were no certainties, no guaranteed return. It was back to taking risks.

Hatch had no real idea what he might find on the Reef. Henri Besancon was convinced that the eighteenth century records about the loss of the *Geldermalsen* were wrong. Through panic, ignorance or a wish to cover up mistakes, the survivors, he believed, had inaccurately plotted the place of disaster. It made more sense for the Dutch East Indiaman to have hit Admiral Stellingwerf. Hatch half-believed Henri. He was half-looking for the"G". But there was a good chance of finding something, and if the whole expedition was fruitless – well, they would have a good time, enjoy some fun diving.

What he did find was beyond anyone's expectations. Quite early on, his divers came across some gleaming blue and white shards on the sea bed. Close by were perfectly preserved items of porcelain. Could this be the *Geldermalsen's* cargo? Hatch was going to Amsterdam on business. His speculative survey of the Admiral Stellingwerf seemed to be paying off. He took some forty of the items to Christie's office there – to have all his theories exploded. He had not found the "Big One." He had, instead, come across a completely unknown seventeenth century Chinese junk. He had discovered the Ming wreck which was to go down in art world history as the "Hatcher collection."

3

Story of a Junk

Talking about it now, Hatch has a soft spot for the Ming porcelain: he prefers it to the *Geldermalsen*. It did not bring in as much money – by the time the Ming cargo had been auctioned at Christie's in Amsterdam, in a series of four sales which stretched from late 1983 to early 1985, it totalled almost two million pounds – but the quality of the porcelain was much higher. If the Nanking ceramics appealed to first-time buyers of Chinese works of art, the Ming excited the connoisseurs. In a way, this parallels the original markets for the two cargoes – the Nanking was aimed at the developing middles classes of eighteenth-century Europe who, for the first time, could afford decent "china". The Ming, dating from just over a century earlier, would have found buyers among a smaller, affluent, upper class.

But the Ming was not only rarer, and much more important from a specialist's viewpoint: it also gave Hatch a taste for Chinese ceramics. Until the discovery of the Ming his interest in old cargoes was financial: they might prove a profitable alternative to the lacklustre

Kraak blue and white (left).

Two transitional blue and white oviform jars and covers (right).

market for salvaged metal from modern ships. But as the blue and white plates, large dishes, bottle vases, water jugs and bowls were hauled to the surface, Hatch found himself drawn to these beautiful examples of long-lost craftsmanship.

Today Hatch is often invited to talk to learned ceramics societies, or to pontificate on television about Chinese porcelain: his knowledge of the subject is constantly expanding. It was the Ming which first excited his enthusiasm and it is pieces from this find (which he kept back from the auction rooms) which form the heart of his own, very fine, collection. He likes to fondle the creamy blue and white vases, which opened up such an exciting new life for him; but at the same time he also likes to find out how much you think they are worth.

The Ming is not only important in being Hatch's first profitable old wreck. It also sparked off a much greater row among experts in Chinese works of art than the *Geldermalsen* cargo. This appeals to Hatch. He likes to contrast his approach to Chinese porcelain with that of the connoisseurs. They might pick up an item, examine it carefully all

A dazzling display of blue and white (left), from dealer Axel Vervoordt.

Transitional blue and white vases.

over, and then, very cautiously, and with much hesitancy, attribute a certain origin, or a possible date, to it. Hatch does not have their expertise, but by producing "irrefutable" dating evidence from his sea-bed finds he feels that he has contributed more to the knowledge of Chinese ceramics in the seventeenth and eighteenth centuries than all the scholars of Europe. Some of them have tried to argue against his evidence, especially in relation to the Ming, but it cannot be doubted that, after Hatcher, some revision of the textbooks on seventeenth-century Chinese porcelain has become essential.

The junk carrying the Ming was discovered in a hundred and thirty feet of water on the Admiral Stellingwerf Reef about a mile from where, a year later, Hatch would make his second, financially more momentous, find. One of the pieces of Mike's porcelain, from the twenty-five thousand or so pieces recovered, carried the date 1643, which confirms the views of the experts that the junk must have sunk around 1645. It was almost certainly a porcelain junk, carrying its merchandise between the Chinese communities of South-East Asia, perhaps from China to Batavia in Java.

There, the more mundane items in the cargo – and there were small tea bowls, sets of saucers and pill boxes by the hundred – might well have found buyers among the local Chinese community, while the higher quality items would have been shipped on to Europe, probably to the Netherlands: in these days the Dutch East India Company used Batavia rather than Canton as the centre for its trade between Europe and the Far East. The junk, like the *Geldermalsen*, must have sunk slowly, for many of the items were still packed in the freight barrels and chests, protected with rice husks. It was a considerable achievement for Hatch and his divers to rescue so much of the delicate cargo, especially as their previous salvaging experience had been limited to tin, copper, and other completely insensitive materials.

Experts are confident that the ship was Asian rather than European, although it had international connections and was, perhaps, even carrying European passengers – a couple of muskets were found, but in too derelict a condition to sell. Among other items recovered with the porcelain were a flat iron, pill boxes, a censer, an ink stone and a gong – all resolutely Chinese – but two pieces of pewter made in Holland – a salt and a jug.

It was the fortuitous business trips of Hatch to Amsterdam which brought the Ming to Christie's. They have an office there which organizes sales of Chinese porcelain, especially blue and white, which has been collected in the Netherlands since the seventeenth century. At first their experts were very cautious about the few dozen pieces Hatch brought to them. They did not doubt they had come from the sea – there were enough barnacles clinging to the pots to confirm that – but Hatch was secretive about where he had actually found them, and good pieces of no great rarity, and with a doubtful provenance, are not popular among buyers. Christie's tagged a hundred of them onto the end of a general sale of Chinese works of art in December 1983. The items were a mixed success – some selling for low prices; some failing to excite any bids whatsoever.

But Hatch was encouraged: he had earned money from the junk and with his divers on "no pay – no cure" (apart from their keep, they earned nothing except their twenty per cent of any saleable finds) he could at last arrange a small distribution of cash. And he knew there was still lots more blue and white to come to the surface.

When Hatch returned with the bulk of the junk's cargo early in 1984 Christie's was forced to sit up and take notice. It decided to play up the romantic origins of the blue and white, but it was still nervous about the reaction of dealers – who were certain to be the main buyers – towards what seemed like a vast quantity of seventeenth-century Ming pouring on to the market. It arranged two sales, testing the market in March, with a follow-up planned, if all went well, in June.

All did go well. The first sale in March echoed the much greater auction that would take place in the same rooms just over two years later when the *Geldermalsen's* hoard came home. Bidders were already less concerned with the visual quality of the blue and white, much of

These Kraak dishes show the variety of the designs.

which was very mundane, than with the documentary significance, and £540,000 was raised, way above the pre-sale forecast. Captain Hatcher was making his name: indeed by the time of the much larger auction in June, Christie's had cast all caution to the wind and were heavily promoting the event as the "Hatcher collection." This time almost £1m. was brought in. They repeated the exercise in February 1985 when Hatch sold off 226 items of higher quality pieces which he had held back.

The sales of the Ming split both the commercial and the academic worlds of Chinese works of art. Some of the dealers were suspicious about the lack of information about the exact location of the wreck and how the cargo had been recovered. They were also critical about Christie's original hesitancy about the true size and importance of the find (although the salesroom was kept in the dark, too, about the quantity) and were not impressed about the quality of the items: many of the dishes were thick, and had been warped in their original firing.

On the other hand they were out-gunned by the small group of dealers who appreciated the opportunity of acquiring vast quantities of blue and white at comparatively low prices. It enabled modern interior decorators to plan rooms in the grand tradition of masses and masses of blue and white porcelain, providing a magnificent backdrop. It would be possible once again to create the porcelain interiors that graced Dutch royal palaces and Hampton Court in London in the late seventeenth century.

In particular dealers such as Axel Vervoordt of Antwerp and Elizabeth Gertz of Dallas, as well as the London dealer David Howard who acquired many of the rarities, succeeded in buying thousands of pieces. Today there are at least four homes in Texas which are ablaze with blue and white, to say nothing of some Arab mansions in England. After the first tentative sale in December these dealers, bidding against each other, had to pay high prices for their stock. Blue and white "Kraak" porcelain plates, a common item, which would go at auctions as a matter of routine for around £500 each, were selling for £4,000 for a pair. A rare peach-shaped wine ewer sold for five times its forecast, at £2,546. In another foretaste of the *Geldermalsen* auction a "transitional" bottle vase of poor quality and covered in barnacles was bought for £700 although Christie's was expecting to get just £50.

This was in March. By the June auction Christie's was bravely organizing the auction of a daunting 15,000 pieces of porcelain, divided into 1,600 lots. Here was an eighteenth century Dutch East India Company sale come to life again. What amazed Christie's, and the antiques trade, was the consistency of the demand. Items had been estimated to sell at the prices they had actually secured at the March sale, but time after time these forecasts were exceeded, and for some pieces, notably wine pots and teapots, prices were climbing even higher. What were reckoned to be riskily large lots – up to 120 small bowls or dishes – were snapped up by those dealers who had belatedly realized that, far from flooding the market, the Ming cargo was acting as a stimulant. The romance of an ancient shipwreck obviously enhanced the value of porcelain. The lesson was taken on board, and Hatch, instead of being a mysterious stranger to be treated with caution, became the hero of Christie's.

Ming en masse. It was used to cover walls with a dazzling blue and white effect.

The dealers who bought early on did very well from the Ming. The three-thousand plates from the find were selling at the auction at six for £400; a year later at the Dorchester Hotel Ceramics Fair in London, which was awash with blue and white from Hatcher, prices were £150 for a single plate. Since, however, they were not individually marked by Christie's, not every plate or bowl marketed as "Hatcher Ming" is the real thing.

Christie's heaved a huge sigh of relief after the final Ming sale. It had got rid of a huge quantity of mainly mediocre seventeenth-century blue and white, often with cracks and unappealing matt surface. It had done so by playing up the dramatic origin of the porcelain, and creating a provenance. And it was greatly helped by the academic controversies which began to whirl around Hatch's find, and which still do. This foot-loose salvager, with little formal education, has managed to set the erudite world of the Chinese ceramics experts by the heels. This is the true importance of the Ming cargo.

The key was the barrel-shaped pot and cover which bore the mark for 1643. Without that, the experts would tentatively have estimated the cargo to date from the early years of the seventeenth century, although there were some odd shapes among it. By confirming the wreck to the mid 1640s, the specialists were contemplating a vast quantity of porcelain from a period of considerable obscurity in Chinese ceramics studies. It was an era when a civil war was raging in China which would overthrow the native Ming Dynasty and disrupt the manufacture and trade in porcelain. Ultimately victory would go to the Manchu warriors from the north, and new artistic tastes and technologies would develop.

So much of the porcelain is what is known as "transitional". Had it been made twenty years earlier, the plates and pots would have been of a much higher quality, but in tumultuous times the porcelain factories

Buddhist lions, holders for joss sticks.

The dated barrel-jar of 1643 which so excited the experts.

could not maintain standards. But if the surfaces were less refined, the decoration suggested the use of woodblock prints which were just then coming into fashion. In particular there was a set of twelve saucer dishes decorated with designs from popular wood blocks of the day which much excited connoisseurs, and the dishes have now disappeared into the best Chinese collections.

The Ming cargo has confirmed that types of porcelain produced in the early years of the seventeenth century were still being manufactured a generation later. In the same way, celadon dishes, usually dated to the sixteenth century, were also obviously being made in substantial quantities many years later, while blanc de chine, which is mainly associated with a later period, was already on the market before 1650. All these discoveries, vital to students of Chinese porcelain, came through Hatch, and in particular through the two dated pieces: it is very, very rare to discover a dated item of between 1640 and 1680, when life in China was back to normal.

So the transitional years in China between Ming and Qing, are being re-interpreted by the experts. For some of them it is proving a chastening experience. In particular the Ashmolean Museum in Oxford might have to change some of the labels on the excellent collection of seventeenth-century porcelain donated to it by the late Mr Gerald Reitlinger. To the surprise of some scholars, the Ashmolean dated many of the items of porcelain that it inherited to sixty years later than

the generally accepted period. There were some blanc de Chine pieces on Hatch's junk, which confirms the view that they were produced earlier in the century, and while the Ashmolean has attempted to attack Hatch for the lack of scientific research he undertook while bringing up the cargo, even suggesting that he might have come across two wrecks, one on top of the other, dating from different periods, the consensus view is that the Ashmolean will have to re-date its blue and white. This was only the most public row to surface with the porcelain: other books are currently being written re-assessing celadon and blue and white on the basis of the firm dating supplied by Hatch.

The best buy at the Ming auctions was undoubtedly the pot which had the cover bearing the cyclical date corresponding to 1643. Christie's, amazingly unaware of its importance, had placed an estimate of around £100 on this lot: it eventually went for around £5,000, and the collector has subsequently turned down much higher offers. Only a year later the last Ming Emperor Chongzhen, was cut down by his guards. The Qing Emperor Shunzhi came to power in Beijing (Peking).

By such events were the periods of Chinese porcelain catalogued. Not any more. The Hatcher junk contained Kraak and Transitional goods in roughly equal quantities. Traditionally Kraak, so called because of the carrackes, the Portuguese ships that first brought the porcelain to Europe, was thought to have gone out of fashion by 1630, to be replaced by Transitional wares. Now Kraak has had its period of manufacture extended by another decade or more – thanks to Hatch. There are also many items which Christie's was unable to catalogue accurately because they did not correspond to either Kraak or Transitional forms. Earlier certainties have become question marks.

The Ming will keep the experts happy for years. They had no idea that such diverse types and qualities of porcelain were still being exported from China during the civil wars. Luxury items, such as wine bowls, stem bowls, tea bowls and the like, still had pretensions towards style, and even the larger pieces – dishes and bowls for meals, covered jars and bottles, censers, urinals and night lights – were often well shaped and painted, mainly in blue and white.

The Nanking cargo would not have been possible without the finding of the junk. Hatch used the money he made to reward his crew and to finance the larger expedition in 1985. Divers pressed him for jobs; Max de Rham was sufficiently convinced to throw in his lot with Hatch and to lend his surveying skills to the venture. Hatch took on board the lesson that buyers need to be convinced of the genuine provenance of finds and he made certain that a member of the crew in 1985 was the photographer John Bremmer, who was most fortuitously on hand to film the actual discovery of the *Geldermalsen*. There could be no doubts about the genuineness of this salvage and Bremmer's video did much to sell the story of the Nanking cargo to the world.

Hatch was still reluctant to give too much away about the actual site he was working. To his way of thinking, anyone with any intelligence should be able to work it out for themselves: it was hardly a tucked-away corner. The Reef was a very well known nautical hazard and in these busy waters there was a constant procession of fishing vessels and other shipping passing him by. But he did not want to attract spoilers after his nasty experience with the *Risdam*.

The discovery and exploitation of the Chinese junk has slipped out of the public consciousness. It excited scholars and collectors but was hardly the stuff to excite the man in the street. Even academics and dealers were slow to appreciate the full significance of the find. The paucity of reaction re-inforced Hatch's decision not to take a marine archaeologist along on the hunt for the "G." There had been some low-key murmurings in academic circles that the junk should have been more slowly and systematically excavated, with as much attention paid to its archaeological significance as to the value of its cargo at auction. But while one lesson was learned from the junk (the need for discoveries to be captured on film to re-assure buyers) another (that attention should be paid to the historical importance of any find) was ignored. Given the short salvaging season in the South China Sea, Hatch believes that the painstaking scholarly approach is impracticable. It forces costs up too high and encourages human predators.

It was very much the same team of divers that left Singapore in March 1985 en route for the Reef. But sailing alongside in his yacht was Max de Rham. And, also very important, Captain Hatcher was commanding a different ship. He had used some of the £1m that he had made from the Amsterdam auctions to buy the *Restless M*, which began life as a Florida-based trawler but which had been rudimentarily converted into a floating home. By a coincidence his new boat could not have a more suitable name. Mike always has been restless; always preferred living off a boat to a land-based home. The appropriateness of the name; its cheapness – less than 200,000 US dollars; and its sturdiness appealed to Hatch. It is likely to stay his flagship for some time.

The *Restless M* is in no way an elegant boat. It looks like a work-horse. Today it is crammed with the latest equipment – with telex machines as well as telephones; with monitors giving the bad weather forecasts, and radar systems that would not disgrace a battleship. The bridge has every necessary gadget to take the fatigue out of navigating.

But while there is no more sophisticated ship of its size in the Far East in its modern technology, the crew are still confined, doubled up for cosiness, into three cabins. Hatch has a grand stateroom, and his own shower, but then he does live most of the time on the *Restless M*. But for Dorian Ball who joined Hatch as a diver in the hunt for the *Geldermalsen*, the first view of his cabin, down in the bilges of the ship, alongside a noisy engine and with a suffocating heat, was horrifying. There are compensations – a spacious lounge with a good selection of video and musical tapes, and a sun deck with a fisherman's seat at the rear. The *Restless M* also carries a good supply of surf-boards for leisure times.

As they sped east and south through the crowded harbour of Singapore, the divers on the *Restless M* had no idea what their expedition might find. They knew the Reef was a graveyard; they had all investigated some of its submerged residents. Hatch, convinced by Henry Besancon's arguments, was hopeful that this time he might come across the *Geldermalsen*. But if it proved elusive there was a good chance that, with Max de Rham's sidescan, they would find some other wreck, another Chinese junk perhaps. And if their luck was completely out there was always the fun diving, the comradeship, the escape from a big city and a frantic world.

The discovery of the junk, coming on top of Hatch's successes with the salvaging of modern wrecks, had inspired confidence in his divers. They were trecking with the most successful underwater recovery man in Asia. They did not know what the next ten weeks would bring but they were pretty certain that they would not come back empty-handed. That they would actually hit upon the elusive *Geldermalsen*, and that its cargo would be miraculously intact, was outside even Hatch's most ambitious hopes.

4

Lost at Sea

On Monday January 3rd, 1752, the *Geldermalsen*, a merchantman of the Dutch East India Company (VOC), is placidly sailing south in the South China Sea on its way home to the Netherlands from Canton which it left fifteen days previously. It carries a cargo of tea and textiles, including raw silk. There is also a large quantity of porcelain on board.

The porcelain, while certainly not regarded as ballast, is the least significant part of the load. Its value to the Dutch East India Company is just over 37,000 guilders, not much more than five per cent of the total worth of the cargo. It is the tea, valued at around 400,000 guilders, which is the big profit-maker from the China trade, followed by the silk and textiles. But Chinese export porcelain is much in demand in Europe, especially among the aspiring middle classes. It pays for its transportation – just.

The *Geldermalsen* is also carrying one other important commodity – gold. Chinese gold is the cheapest in Asia and is much in demand at the bustling port of Batavia (now Jakarta in Indonesia). The merchants there use it to buy textiles from India which they then trade for spices. The gold will be off-loaded from the *Geldermalsen* in the Sunda Strait onto another vessel which will take it further south to Batavia.

Although the *Geldermalsen* is barely five years old her new captain, thirty-three-year-old Jan Morel, who took charge of her in Canton, is not happy with her condition. He has been forced to acquire spare parts, new compasses and maps. He has also instructed the other ship meeting her in the Sunda Strait to carry an extra twenty barrels of drinking water for the *Geldermalsen*, for her own containers are already going mouldy. But on this particular day the sea is calm, the weather good, and the one hundred and twelve people on board are learning to cope with a diet of rice and beans and the tedium of a five-month journey to the Cape of Good Hope, where new provisions can be secured.

It should be a trouble free passage. The *Geldermalsen* is one of the newest and finest of the Dutch East Indiamen, built as recently as 1746 for the Zeeland Chamber of the VOC and named after the family

A Dutch East Indiaman of the same type as the Geldermalsen. *A copper engraving.*

manor of its director Jan Van Borsele. It is one hundred and fifty feet long, forty two feet wide, eighteen feet in draft, and weighs 11,000 metric tons. It has three masts and is armed with thirty one cannons. The *Geldermalsen* has not seen its homeland since it was launched. It has been employed on the profitable eastern trade between India, Batavia and China.

The crew, also new recruits to the *Geldermalsen*, are a mixed bunch, mainly Dutch but with sixteen Englishmen who have signed up for the voyage in their eagerness to get back to Europe quickly. There is also a paying passenger, another Englishman, Richard Bagge, who is anxious to get to Batavia and who expects to trans-ship with the gold. It will prove a pious hope.

The *Geldermalsen* has been making good progress, aided by the north-west monsoon pushing it on. Captain Morel is anxious to get back to Holland as soon as possible. Although of German origins he married a Dutch wife three years previously and is eager to see the son born to him while he has been at sea. At about four in the afternoon Morel comes on deck and questions the boatswain, Van Dijk about the dangerous Geldrias reefs: have they been sited yet? Yes, to the north-west, is the answer, and Morel orders a change of course. The *Geldermalsen* turns to the south.

At six, watchman Jean Delia and two young crewmen climb the mast to look for land. Nothing can be seen, but all is peaceful, all is calm. A few minutes later, just after sunset, another boatswain, Urbanus Urbani, a Corsican who has been checking the anchors, suddenly catches sight of breakers, the last thing you expect to see on the open ocean just south of the Equator. The *Geldermalsen* is about to hit a reef, the notorious Admiral Stellingwerf Reef, which hides just below the surface of the sea over twelve miles from the island of Bintan.

Morel quickly takes charge, shouting out orders. "Tighten the mainsheet! Back the mainsail! Slacken the mizzen sheet!" The *Geldermalsen* lurches, and loosens itself from the Reef. But in the confusion the starboard main jib sheet has been cut and the ship drifts slowly backwards on to the Reef again. This time there is no escape. With a crash the main mast comes tumbling down, the rudder is torn away by the sea, and inexorably the *Geldermalsen* starts to fill with water. Morel orders the anchor to be dropped. The big day anchor tries to stabilize the ship but its line breaks. A second, smaller, anchor meets the same fate. The *Geldermalsen* by this time has come off the Reef but is drifting south into the night with the crew vainly at the pumps trying to staunch the rising sea in the bilges.

Morel orders the main anchor to be dropped and this brings the ship to a shuddering halt. But it is obviously sinking and the captain, still calm, orders the barge and the long boat to be lowered into the sea. He gets the sick among the crew into the barge and tells Van Dijk and five other sailors to man the long boat.

But, as the *Geldermalsen* starts slowly to sink in the darkness, confusion breaks out. In all probability old scores are being settled between crew and officers, between Dutchmen and Englishmen. No doubt the gin and the beer containers have been looted, with any other portable goods. By midnight the foredeck is half submerged, with Morel and the surviving crew – some will have already been killed by the falling mast – huddled on the aftdeck shouting to the sailors who have made it to the barge and long boat. Many will have drowned in the attempt: in the mid-eighteenth century few sailors could swim. Urbani is given some charts and a compass by Morel and with another quartermaster, who has tied more charts to his back, they jump for the barge which by this time contains around twenty men. Another dozen

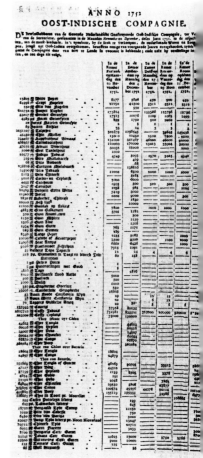

Announcement of a VOC sale in 1752 – the Geldermalsen *cargo is of course missing, but that of the* Amstelveen *fetched high prices.*

have managed to reach Van Dijk in the long boat. All night the shouting and the screaming continues but the currents keep the small boats away from the mother ship.

By dawn the *Geldermalsen* has disappeared.

For the survivors there is a hazardous journey to Batavia which they reach in eight days. For some of the thirty-two it has been a vain endeavour and they die of fever on land. For others of the survivors, especially the boatswain Christoffel Van Dijk, their problems are only just beginning. Significantly, none of the Englishmen reaches land; nor any officers; nor the English merchant. The authorities are suspicious, especially of the actions of Van Dijk who had been on watch during the afternoon before the disaster. How could the *Geldermalsen* have hit the well-charted Geldrias Reefs? And, most pressing of all for the tribunal set up to question the survivors, what has happened to the gold?

Van Dijk always claimed complete ignorance of any gold being on board the ship. Another survivor, the captain's steward, known only as Arnold, gave evidence that Morel ordered him and another crewman to take a very heavy trunk from his cabin and bring it on deck. Just as they were attaching it to a side-rope to swing it over-board, the *Geldermalsen* went down. Arnold is one of the few sailors to reach the small boats.

His account neatly dovetails with Hatcher's discovery of the gold. Hatcher came across it at the end of his investigation outside the hull and among the bricks washed out from the galley area. This suggests that the gold was being off-loaded at the last minute and the weight of the chest was too much for struggling men on a capsizing ship. But if Van Dijk's name is cleared at last, he still suffered for his survival: when he was once more employed by the Dutch East India Company it was as third master earning fourteen guilders a month as against the twenty-six guilders he received as boatswain.

The loss of the *Geldermalsen* – ship, cargo, gold – cost the Dutch East India Company almost 900,000 guilders. There was some compensation in the fact that its sister ship, the *Amstelveen* , which had left Canton three weeks earlier to arrive back home in July 1752, now carried all the Chinese goods to reach the Netherlands that summer. As a result prices soared, and the *Amstelveen* turned in a profit of over a hundred per cent in the autumn auction, twenty-three per cent more than the Company had made in the previous year.

Even so, the loss of the *Geldermalsen*was a grievous blow to the Dutch East India Company, which had seen its profits fall after 1751 because of foreign competition and a decline in the quality of the tea on offer. But if it was a blow to the Company it has proved a most

The shipyard at Middelburg where the Geldermalsen *was built in 1746.*

tremendous coup for historians – to say nothing of Captain Hatcher and Christie's.

For relatively few Dutch East Indiamen went down in the eighteenth century – the *Enkhuijzen* in 1741; the *Vreedenhoff* and the *Abbekerk* in 1778; the *Zeeploeg* in 1779, and some smaller craft in the 1780s. It is very unlikely that the wrecks of any of these traders will be discovered, and even more unlikely that their cargoes will be as intact as that of the *Geldermalsen*, whose slow, smooth, sinking may have been a catastrophe for the crew, in that it fed false hope, but has been a bonus for modern salvagers.

The painstaking research of Dr Christiaan Jorg of Groningen University, the expert on the Dutch East India Company, has knitted together the comprehensive surviving records of the Company with the discoveries from the wreck of the *Geldermalsen*. There are some mysteries, some missing links between what was on the manifest of the ship and what was found beneath the sea, but there was little doubt about the real identity of the ship even before confirmation came in the form of the bell, with the launch date 1747; the VOC marks on the ship's cannon; and the final proof, the initials F.B., referring to the

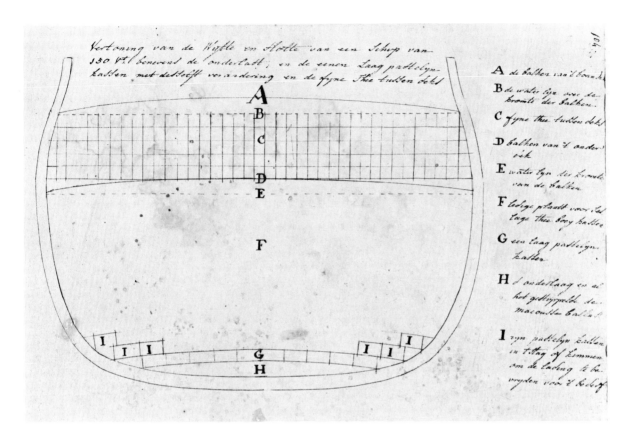

A sketch for the stowage of a VOC ship. H indicates ballast; G and I porcelain chests; F six layers of tea chests; C the fine tea; and D, B and A the joisting.

ship's surgeon, uncovered among medicine bottles when Hatcher made one last dive in 1986 to clinch the matter.

Dr Jorg has looked at the evidence produced at the inquiry into the sinking of the *Geldermalsen* and compared it with the archaeological evidence Hatcher gathered from the wreck and has been able to absolve Van Dijk of any nefarious practices. The boatswain's report of the disaster holds true – although there are still some gold bars unaccounted for. Jorg has also been able to balance the details of the cargo listed in the records with the porcelain finally brought to Amsterdam so many years late. The tea, of course, was gone, but its existence, packed among the tablewares, contributed greatly to the preservation of the porcelain.

Jorg bemoans the speed with which the *Geldermalsen* was excavated, and, undoubtedly, some historical evidence was destroyed, but rarely can a find have so fleshed out the bare details of musty documents. The thousands of people who gazed in wonder at the stacks of blue and white porcelain – plates and bowls, cups and saucers, flagons and vomit cups in Amsterdam in 1986 – were sharing an experience with their forefathers of over two hundred years ago. But what exactly was in the "Nanking cargo", and why has it excited both historians and the

The Canton water front around 1770, showing the presence of the European factors (above).

A dinnerplate of around 1740, showing VOC ships anchored off Cape Town.

competing factions of the fine art market-dealers, collectors and connoisseurs?

The Dutch East India Company had been formed in 1602 and by the eighteenth century was at the height of its powers. It had over two-hundred ships flying its flag and employed 120,000 seamen, to say nothing of 17,000 soldiers and many clerks, book-keepers, hospital staff, etc. Its great entrepot centre for the East was the port of Batavia, in Java, and for years the authorities there rivalled their ostensible masters in Amsterdam in influence. But gradually, while most East Indiamen still put into Batavia on the outward journey from Europe to China, on their return they sailed directly from Canton. By doing so, their tea, the major commodity, arrived back in the Netherlands that much fresher. Tea drinking had become the great fashionable craze after 1700, filtering down from the upper classes to the growing numbers of the middle class. Merchants from England, France and Denmark had established themselves in Canton to superintend the tea trade and by 1730 the Dutch were there, too.

The Chinese strictly controlled operations: they liked the profits but not the Europeans. Everything was channelled through Canton, but foreigners could not own land there; the ships' crews could not even go on shore; and there were to be no women. At certain times of the year, especially in the spring, even the merchants were banished from China. A routine was soon established. The Dutch East Indiamen sailed from Batavia in the summer, usually arriving off China a month later. They would always be carrying gifts for Chinese officials: when the *Geldermalsen* arrived at Canton on July 21, 1751, the cost of these, plus import duties, worked out at over 45,000 guilders.

The *Geldermalsen* was carrying tin and cotton, which it sold for a profit of 75,000 guilders. This sum, with profits accumulated by the Company in earlier years, was used to defray expenses and to buy the return cargo, which was naturally built around tea, the green or Emperor's tea, and the cheaper black tea. By the time it was sold in the Netherlands the tea would be providing the Company with a ninety per cent return on its capital expenditure. In addition the *Geldermalsen* was to bring back silk and textiles, plants of rhubarb and ginger, lacquerwork – and the special assignment of gold for Batavia. There was also one other commodity which had become much more prominent since 1730 – porcelain.

There was a burgeoning demand in Europe for ordinary Chinese porcelain by those same middle classes that had taken to tea. For the first time modestly placed people could afford to eat and drink off porcelain plates, dishes, bowls, tea and coffee sets. The company was only interested in the mass market, in buying bulk from the porcelain dealers in Canton and selling, at a profit of up to a hundred per cent, to the wholesalers of the Netherlands. Top quality porcelain, and special commissions for wealthy European customers, were left to the private traders. The porcelain was put at the bottom of the *Geldermalsen*, over two-hundred crates of it in all, to stiffen the ballast and also to act as a firm base for the important commodity, the tea.

The ship was meticulously loaded. Over the original ballast, a layer of Pearl River gravel is raked flat, and on top of this is placed the planks of valuable calliatour and sappan wood. Then the heavy wooden crates with the porcelain are laid to form an even floor. Finally the most valuable items, the tea, packed in tin-lined wooden boxes, will be carefully carried on, with the silk and other choice goods. In all it takes over two months to complete the loading of the *Geldermalsen*.

In theory the merchants working for the Dutch East India Company in Canton would have a list of the porcelain wanted in the Netherlands, but in practice they often had to exercise their own judgement, stocking up with what was readily at hand. The Company's instructions were based on what had sold well at the Dutch auctions a year previously so that by the time the shipment arrived in Europe it was geared to the public taste of three years before. For 1752, according to the Dutch records, the main requests were for 225,303 pieces of porcelain and fifty dinner services of 161 pieces. The desired designs were blue and white and what is now known as Chinese Imari, as well as brown ware, also known as Batavia ware, and enamelled, a new process whereby designs were added to white porcelain at workshops in Canton, thus improving the chances of the merchants obtaining more exactly what their customers wanted.

Not everything ordered from Zeeland, the chapter of the Dutch East India Company which controlled the *Geldermalsen* and its intended destination, was loaded on to the ships, and sometimes the cargo carried on board was quite contrary to orders. The cupboard garnitures, coffee pots and milk jugs clearly requested do not seem to have been available, while other items that the Company had obviously found to be poor sellers, notably butter dishes and vomit cups (a useful recent innovation designed as an accessory to over-lavish meals) were packed in profusion although no more had been ordered. It seems possible that the Canton merchants did not receive the Company's detailed list for 1752 and just filled the ship with the type of porcelain that they had despatched in the previous year. After all, porcelain was not the most vital ingredient of the cargo and time was pressing. It had to be put on board before the tea arrived.

In addition, the *Geldermalsen* would carry private trade goods, what we might call the "duty frees", sent on board by Canton merchants to friends and relatives back in Europe. It is these, along with the personal possessions of the crew, which provided some of the more interesting finds from the wreck.

By matching the *Geldermalsen* manifest with what Hatcher was bringing up from the Reef, Dr Jorg was able to advise on the salvaging. It was at his urging that a second, speedy, dive was undertaken to look for the ship's bell and the bronze cannon. The final pieces of the jigsaw had been found. The very fact that the porcelain lacked items listed on the manifest while including other pieces has told historians much of the day-to-day trading problems, over long distances and with unreliable communications, in the mid-eighteenth century.

Dr Jorg cannot hide his irritation that a more meticulous archaeological search was not made. He was grateful for the discovery of a candlestick and one is listed among the cabin goods. But was it a candlestick used by Captain Morel and Richard Bagge as they mulled over their evening brandy? If its exact location on the sea bed had been passed on more information about social life on board a merchantman would have been collated.

If the actual trawl for crews' possessions has proved disappointing – the odd wine jug, an unusual porcelain figure – the recovery of the bronze cannons and the ship's bell, the latter generously given by Hatcher and de Rham to a Dutch museum, has produced some solid objects for research. It was the finding of the gold which created the greatest sensation, and sparked off the publicity bonanza which was so vital to the success of the sale. Hatcher was very lucky here. Dutch East Indiamen carried gold on the return to Europe for just twenty-five years after 1735 and only two "lost" ships had gold on board – the *Enkhuizen* and the *Geldermalsen*. There should have been 147 ingots in all. Perhaps some are still at the bottom of the ocean; perhaps some were concealed by the survivors. Even so the 126 pieces of finest Chinese gold, of a type never seen in modern times, provided the romantic basis on which to construct the Hatcher legend.

The gold caught the headlines and the popular imagination; the porcelain ensured that the *Geldermalsen* will go down as one of the turning points in marine salvaging. It is inconceivable that such a vast quantity of Chinese porcelain will ever again be recovered from the past. By the nature of things, when ships go down their cargoes are shaken to bits; if they survive, the sea carries out its destructive tasks. Thanks to the tea which solidified into a thick protective layer over the porcelain (and proved a terrible hazard to the divers as it was disturbed), here was an almost complete haul of Chinese export procelain which, thanks to Dr Jorg, could be dated very precisely. It has proved a research bonanza for the historian and the ceramics expert.

Stages in the production of
porcelain – firing, painting,
transporting and selling – in the
late eighteenth century.

Weighing tea chests in Canton around 1780. The VOC monogram is clearly visible.

It would be foolish to pretend that the porcelain saved from the *Geldermalsen* is of the kind that excites the most refined connoisseurs, or musuem curators – although the British Museum is happy to display some of the wares in recognition of the popular appeal of its recovery. The best examples of Chinese creative genius were sent through the private trade, and destined to grace the homes of the rich: often they carried the armorial crests of their noble European purchasers. This was a cargo of "department store" china, the common blue and white monochrome and enamelled tablewares which were the basic make-weight of a returning merchantman to Europe in the century before 1790 when over-supply, wars, changes in taste, and the development of European porcelain factories brought a quick end to the trade. There is nothing at all special about the pieces from the *Geldermalsen*. They are often quite crudely made, their backs rough, destined for everyday use.

Such items appear at fine art auctions and in antique dealers shops with price tags that rarely top £100. Hence the apprehension at Christie's when it was confronted with the task of offering over 160,000 such pieces to a dormant market.

The porcelain was virtually all potted at Jingdezhen, in Jiangzi province,where over a million people were employed in its production. There is no night in the city – the fire-lit ovens ensure perpetual light. It would then be taken to Nanking for trans-shipment, often by canal, to the warehouses of the Hong merchants on the docks of Canton. Europeans mistakenly believed the porcelain was actually produced in Nanking, and was thus designated "Nanking" or "Nankeen" in the advertisements of the eighteenth century: Christie's decided to revive the brand name.

Most of the pieces from the *Geldermalsen* are decorated with designs very familiar to specialists. Both the Europeans and the Chinese were conservative in their taste – more imaginative works were best left to the private trade. It suited the Chinese to turn out thousands upon thousands of plates, tureens, bowls, in familiar and, presumably, popular sizes and with standard designs taken from Chinese native block-printed books – the scholars in deep conversation, the graceful ladies in their gardens, the pagodas set against mysterious landscapes, sprays of flowers, a fisherman hauling his net: all these famous images abound in the Hatcher and De Rham find.

The same designs appear over a wide range of items: the Europeans of the eighteenth century obviously liked to have matching sets. Christie's re-assembled the sets for the sale, while also offering individual pairs of tureens, condiment pots, etc, to suit collectors with more modest budgets. By far the largest element in the cargo was the tea bowls and saucers: the teapots in varying shapes and sizes were rarer. In all there were 80,000 tea bowls and saucers in twenty-five different designs. Most have underglaze blue patterns, and despite their long immersion in sea water they came up bright and lustrous. Unfortunately the enamelled wares were more badly affected and in many cases the enamel was washed off.

One surprise for the experts was the large number of pieces with brown glaze exteriors, mainly among the tea bowls and saucers. This was not very popular in Europe, judging by the relatively few items that have survived. By chance they were discovered on the only other important merchantman of the period to be excavated: the *Goteborg* which sank as it negotiated the entrance to Gothenburg harbour in 1745. Perhaps the brown glaze became associated with bad luck.

If the abundance of the brown ware was unexpected, there were other mysteries from the cargo, still unresolved. What are we to make of the vomit pots, of which almost 500 were recovered? They are very rare. Indeed some specialists prefer to think of them as chamber pots for children. Perhaps they served two purposes. They first appeared in 1745 and were not long in fashion. They are very desirable for today's collector.

Hatcher also seems to have proved conclusively the difference between tea and coffee bowls – the latter are slightly larger. The relative lack of teapots compared with bowls and saucers is a small mystery, as is the absence of sugar bowls and tea caddies. But in the years up to 1752, most Dutch East Indiamen were arriving in Europe with at least 100,000 items for tea drinking so perhaps the market was becoming saturated.

And still the items came up – chocolate cups and saucers, milk bowls, dinner plates, soup plates, butter dishes, cuspidors (for spitting) and beer mugs – in three sizes the largest holding two pints. In all 681 beer mugs were recovered; inevitably the divers held on to some as personal mementoes.

Not everything salvaged had been destined for the mass market in Zeeland. There were over 1,000 pieces of coarser porcelain, which would have been off-loaded for the less sophisticated customers of the Cape, forefathers of the Boers of South Africa. There were also almost 400 objects of rather special porcelain, gifts for friends, or the items carried by the crew to sell privately – such transactions, on a limited scale, were allowed by the Company. Among the tablewares is a plate decorated in blue and white with a river landscape: on one side of the river there seems to be a church portrayed. This pattern has never been seen before and was perhaps a one-off commission.

The connoisseurs, while unimpressed by the mass of the Nanking cargo, were excited by the sixty-eight porcelain figures recovered. These include a dancing couple, lacking their heads, but obviously inspired by a German original; a smiling boy, minus his shirt; horses and cranes. That standards did not slip too far on board is suggested by the survival of two shaving bowls, made of Japanese Imari. Captain Morel might well have gone fresh-faced to his death.

It is the figures which have most excited historians. The rarest are those with wash-blue details – some ladies, dignitaries, boys and horses. Until Hatcher's and De Rham's discovery they had been dated by experts to the end of the eighteenth century. The figures in green and red robes are considered by Colin Sheaf of Christie's to be the only surviving examples of their type.

It was a mammoth task transporting the porcelain from the Far East to Amsterdam. There a team of girls meticulously cleaned each item,

A merchant inspects the tea.

although the decision was taken early on to leave some pieces with their barnacles and other accretions intact. There were, of course, some breakages while the 160,000 plus articles were divided up into lots, but not enough to cause a scandal.

This was not the first time that Christie's had prepared an auction of Chinese blue and white porcelain. The company was founded by James Christie in 1766 and a year later was offering a "Nanking" table service, including tureens and dishes, seventy-four plates, twelve soup plates, and much more. Hundreds of sales of Chinese porcelain have followed, three or four times a year in London alone in recent times. But never has there been an auction on such a massive scale and never had Christie's, with the full support of Mike Hatcher, mounted such a costly, comprehensive and sophisticated promotional campaign. So vast was the find that there was a real possibility that it could land on the market with a very dull thud. Only by creating new potential customers could this be avoided.

5

Do I Hear Ten Million Pounds?

At 10.30 on the morning of April 28, 1986, John Gloyne, manager of Christie's saleroom in Amsterdam, mounted the rostrum in the blue and white bedecked ballroom of the Hilton Hotel and started the first of eleven sessions to dispose of the 2, 746 lots in the Nanking cargo. He had a packed audience.

There was room for 1,000 but so great was the interest in the auction that hundreds more were squeezed in around the sides and at the back. On hand was a support auctioneer to take any bids from late arrivals. Every serious buyer had been issued with one of the 5,000 numbered paddles in exchange for their name and address: if anyone wished to bid he simply held high the paddle, thus removing the perennial worry that an inadvertent sneeze or a tug of the ear might be mistaken by the auctioneer for a bid.

Seated in the front row were Mike Hatcher, Max de Rahm, Mr Ong and some of the divers, eager to discover how the objects that they had

Twenty thousand people queued to view the Nanking cargo in Amsterdam.

The build-up to the sale.

The media out in force (above).

Mr and Mrs Ong, with Hatch, seem happy with the prices (left).

Dealers take it seriously, as do the telephone bidders (right).

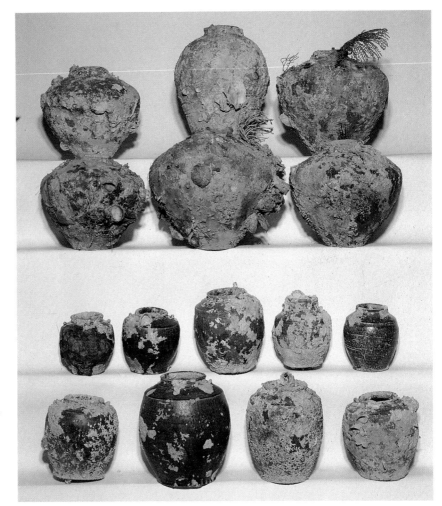

Some of the pieces carried the legacy of their centuries on the sea bed. They were bought as abstract works of art (right).

At the telephones: Colin Sheaf, Mark Wrey, Hetti Jongsma, James Spencer.

Auctioning a dinner service: John Gloyne (near left). Hugo Morley-Fletcher (above).

brought up from the South China Sea with so much toil and strain would convert into hard currency. The first lot was a German stoneware jug made around 1750 and probably originally containing beer for thirsty crewmen. It was encrusted with sea debris and carried an estimate of around 1,000 Dutch guilders or £250.

Within seconds the bids were pouring in, quickly exceeding Christie's cautious estimate, and finally stopping at 11,000 guilders. The buyer was Mike Hatcher. The jug was the first item he had personally brought up from the wreck of the *Geldermalsen* and he was determined to retain it as a memento. He had got the auction off to a good start.

There followed five days of intense excitement. Every lot sold, on average, at prices four or five times its estimate. At the end of Friday Christie's had disposed of almost 160,000 pieces of porcelain and 126

There were 80,000 tea bowls and saucers to find homes for.

Chinese gold ingots for a total of thirty-seven million guilders, or ten million pounds. Christie's had cautiously estimated the sale to bring in three million pounds. "Hatcher fever" took over Amsterdam. By the end of the first day, sharp-nosed dealers were offering items from the sale, all marked with their lot number and a Christie's provenance, in their antique shops at a generous premium, usually twice the purchase price. There were parties; there was the start of dealing between successful buyers and those who had sat on their hands too long; there was even a Hatcher cocktail, suitably blue, available in the Hilton Hotel.

Dealers shook their heads in wonder. Here was a vast quantity of rather second-rate Chinese export porcelain, often with chips and cracks, which had lost its enamel after long exposure under the sea, selling for incredible prices. It was not as if the market for Chinese export porcelain was particularly buoyant at the time.

Yet every day prices rocketed beyond their forecasts. On the Monday Bernheimer, a major dealer in London and Munich, paid £31,351 for a pair of dishes with the blue and white "fish" pattern which were estimated at around £3,000. Mr Ong, not to be out-matched, invested £28,216 of what was bound to be a healthy return from his investment in just one dish which had been expected to sell for less than £2,000.

But the really remarkable session was to follow on Monday evening when the 125 gold bars went under the hammer. The saleroom had never offered anything like them before and confined its estimates to the prevailing price of gold in New York. In the event bidders went crazy for the unusual shoe-shaped ingots – a shape signifying wealth in China – and one three-hundred gram lot sold for £53,297, as against a bullion value of around £2,000. Once again Mr Ong was in there bidding, acquiring his gold bar for £40,756. Max de Rham bought two

Tea pots in every shape and size – and condition.

A blue and white dinner service (right).

shoes – one for each of his children – and another of the team, Nick Bond, also invested in a bar.

By the Tuesday the "Hatcher factor", the desperate desire to acquire a memento of this romantic recovery operation, was in full flow, and a barnacle-encrusted metal sphere, so covered with marine sediment that it was barely distinguishable as a cannon ball, sold for £7,567; it was down in the catalogue with a £400 estimate. It went to a French collector who wanted it as an example of abstract art.

On Wednesday the better quality porcelain was on offer and the serious dealers got down to compete for the large dinner services. Bidding was fast and furious, and the price of £219, 459 – which was paid for one service, consisting of a hundred and forty-four dinner plates, a hundred and forty-four soup plates, twelve salt cellars, four tureens, plus other dishes – was, not surprisingly, a record sum for any dinner service. The price was four times the top estimate.

By Thursday a routine had been established. In all, seven Christie's auctioneers took their places successively at the rostrum, guiding an audience which never dwindled in size through each session of around two hundred and fifty lots. Although there were in the room many new faces who had never attended an auction before, the pace of the selling did not falter and the sessions rarely exceeded two-and-a-half hours. By the fourth day, it was accepted as almost routine when an unexciting pair of blue and white butter tubs sold for £10,032, or twenty-two times their high estimate.

If there was going to be a difficult day it would be Friday when around 80,000 tea bowls and saucers arrived for dispersal. Could there

Blue and white butter tubs and a pair of underglaze blue and enamelled teapots (left).

The cheapest items in the sale – the Batavian bamboo and peony pattern tea bowl and saucer (right).

be enough buyers to absorb such a vast quantity of old china? Of course. Christie's had cleverly split them up into lots of varying sizes to suit the broadest possible range of demand. And the demand was there.

There were some interesting variations in the prices, especially among the cheapest items the Batavian ware bowls, brown on the outside and with a bamboo and peony pattern in the interior. The less affluent buyers were bidding furiously against each other for the smallest sized lots of twelve bowls and saucers: they sold at the start for 4,500 guilders, against a top pre-sale estimate of 600 guilders. With buyers' commission of sixteen per cent added on, it worked out at roughly £100 or slightly more for each bowl and saucer.

But, a dozen or so lots later, forty-eight bowls and saucers in groups were going for sums which brought the unit price down to under £30 a set. The price stayed at roughly this level for the lots of seventy-two sets, but the real bargains were claimed by the dealers competing for lots with a hundred and forty-four sets – by now the unit price was around £20.

Rather surprisingly the biggest lots of all – 1,000 tea bowls and saucers – selling for 80,000 guilders, represented a rise again in the unit price to nearer £30 a set. The same pattern was maintained for the bowls and saucers with the Pagoda riverscape design: the first, small, lots went for very high prices; then there was a dip around the medium-sized lots; and then a slight rise in the unit price among the very largest lots.

It was, of course, dealers, sometimes joining financial forces, who were investing in the large lots and getting the bargains. Individuals going for the smaller sets were paying more. But within a few weeks all would be contemplating bargains on their dining-tables or in their retail display cabinets.

To succeed at the auction, the buyers with limited resources often had to use their initiative. Mrs Janet Wain, who owns, with her husband, a small antique shop at Tetbury in the west of England spent two fruitless days squashed at the back of the hall constantly being

An underglaze blue and white dish (above) *and a blue and white soup plate* (right).

out-bid by the heavy brigade. She got together with two strangers in a similar plight and they pooled their resources to secure a large lot. The next day Mrs Wain was offering sixty pieces of Nanking at her shop at prices ranging from £135 to £260.

By Friday night Christie's was contemplating its records – a record total for any sale in Holland; a record for any porcelain or decorative art sale; the biggest sale of modern times; the second highest total from any Christie's auction; record prices for a gold bar at auction, for a dinner service; and any number of records for individual items.

Immortals and Demons.

For Christie's the records meant little. What mattered was that a terrific gamble had come off and, at a difficult time in its history, it had attracted a cascade of favourable publicity. Everything had gone smoothly. Christie's was also considerably richer. The exact deal it made with Hatcher for handling the auction is a secret. In normal circumstances, a saleroom charges the seller ten per cent of the "hammer" price. For major items – and there has been nothing as major as the Hatcher cargo – so intense is the competition between Christie's and its arch rival Sotheby's to secure the sale that a much lower percentage fee is negotiated. The saleroom will also undertake the horrendous organizational and promotional costs. In this case Christie's probably received less than five per cent of the ten million pounds. But in terms of publicity alone all the effort was more than worthwhile.

While Christie's congratulated itself on a major tactical achievement, Hatcher and his crew were contemplating another fortune but by far their biggest to date. Only he knows how much it cost to raise the cargo of the *Geldermalsen*, but when all the expenses are met he will still have the best part of four million pounds for his efforts. His ten-man crew share around two million – but received no wages while working on the salvaging. There are generous percentages for his close circle of associates especially, Max de Rham and Mr Ong. Another major beneficiary was the Dutch Government. It is considered to be the legal heir to the lost Dutch East Indiaman and creamed off ten per cent.

But if there were celebrations in Amsterdam on May 2, there was also the realization that things could have mapped out very differently. Even during the week of the sale there were minor storms: it was disconcerting for Mike Hatcher to receive a phone call from his mother who had put him into care forty-four years previously. She had seen the publicity about the sale and decided to get in touch. There was, in the event, no communication between the two.

A bigger threat to the success of the sale had been the strong opposition mounted towards it by the Rijksmuseum and its curator of marine archaeology, Mr Bas Kit. He considered that the *Geldermalsen* had been salvaged too quickly, with all the concentration on bringing up the saleable cargo at the expense of serious historical investigation of the site. He called a press conference to publicize what he considered the inadequate funding of marine archaeology by the Dutch government but when Mike Hatcher attempted to put his point of view he was refused entry. "We fear that in the rush of romantic excitement part of the national heritage will be lost", said Kist. The Risjksmuseum refused to take any part in the bidding.

In the event, the Risjksmuseum's disapproval had no effect on the auction. It was just one more obstacle to overcome and, by late April, Hatcher and Christie's thought they were pretty adept at surmounting problems. The sale of the Nanking cargo had been the great event of the art world in 1986, but there had been no guarantee that it would be such a success when it was first mooted little more than six months previously. The ten million outcome was the result of a very clever marketing campaign for which the credit can be shared between Hatcher and the Christie's press office, and in particular young Mark Wrey.

Hatcher had realized, after the controversy over his recovery of the seventeenth century blue and white porcelain from the junk, that when, or if, he found the *Geldermalsen* he had to make a detailed visual record of its salvaging. So photographer John Bremmer was invited on board, and his video film and photographic work of the divers operating on the sea bed, discovering fresh items, and bringing them to the surface, became an important element in the selling of the Nanking. Max de Rham was also an enthusiastic underwater photographer and many of the stills were his work.

As soon as he had discovered a second old wreck, Hatcher had also contacted Christie's man in the Far East, James Spencer. It was too early to state categorically that Hatcher and de Rham had found the *Geldermalsen* — that proved a long and agonizing task and involved another diving session on the wreck in early 1986 before proof positive was furnished — but obviously a most important discovery had been

Hatch fields a question at the press conference.

made. It was Spencer who helped to persuade Hatcher to dispose of the porcelain through Christie's. Not everything had gone smoothly over the earlier auctions and Sotheby's was making friendly noises. But in the end Hatcher, a great believer in loyalty, stuck with Christie's and Amsterdam.

One of the attractions of Amsterdam, apart from the over-riding appeal of the porcelain coming home to the country of its destination some two hundred and thirty-five years late, was that the Christie's saleroom there was not too busy to cope with the tremendous task of cleaning, putting into lots, and warehousing what was the biggest quantity of porcelain to be offered on the market at any one time.

But Christie's in Amsterdam could not cope with the marketing. That task was assigned to London. Mark Wrey immediately appreciated the importance of the film footage. It brought the whole adventure to life. The dangers, the complications, even the tedium of raising delicate, rare, and historic items from the depths of a treacherous sea can hardly be imagined in Europe. The film would form the basis of selling the Hatcher/de Rham achievement; it coated the enterprise with colour and romance.

For the second time in its history Christie's produced a video for an auction. It was based on Bremner's film footage, and was sent to important dealers; it was also on constant show at salerooms in London, New York and Amsterdam. In all, four hundred videos were made. In late January, at a well-orchestrated press conference in

Provincial blue and white saucer dish, with freely painted dragon. One of twelve (above far left).

Large blue and white deep dish, with four exotic fan-tailed fish (above left).

Underglaze blue and enamelled cylindrical mugs, with tree peonies. About 1750 (below left).

White glazed pheasant on pierced rockwork (right).

Chamber pots (below).

Henri Besancon (left) *inspects the bell of the* Geldermalsen, *with Harts Nystad, Christie's Amsterdam chairman.*

Amsterdam before the world's journalists and TV crews, and with the film the feature of the presentation, the Nanking cargo was launched on the market.

The designation, "The Nanking Cargo", was the inspiration of Colin Sheaf, head of Christie's Chinese department. Nanking was the main distribution point for Chinese porcelain destined for Europe and had a suitably oriental and exotic sound. It was also wonderfully unspecific, for at this stage Christie's still had little hard information about the ship. But with the presence at the press conference of Hatcher, the film, some of the porcelain, and a cannon, flown in that week from Singapore and one of the last items to be brought up from the deep, the announcement generated enough publicity to re-assure Christie's.

It was absolutely essential to appeal to new collectors, to people who had never bought Chinese works of art in the past and who had never imagined they ever would. To most serious collectors the Nanking cargo was pretty basic stuff, certainly not worth paying a premium price to obtain. But for thousands of individuals throughout the world, and for social clubs, restaurants, hotels, Women's Institutes, obtaining an item from this long-lost merchantman became an obsession.

As the story flashed from Europe to the US, so the enquiries started to arrive. Hatcher threw himself with enthusiasm into selling his find, giving lectures in London, Amsterdam, Singapore and New York, and popping up on television and radio shows. The big New York department stores were approached and offered the porcelain for a pre-sale window display. They turned down the suggestion. Later Bloomingdales was to take it for an autumn promotion.

Two bronze cannon from the wreck – the VOC marking helped to confirm that it was the Geldermalsen.

1656 – the number of the cannon; another clue to its origin.

By March Christie's (and Hatcher) were breathing more easily. There had been a record number of pre-sale bids for any auction – over 130,000 of them. Most were hopelessly too low and were for the small lots. Each had to be laboriously processed. By this stage the auction was obviously going to sell well – but at what price level?

Christie's kept its estimates low – Hatcher was always more confident that his find would touch the popular nerve. The main worries were concentrated on the gold, which Christie's had never sold in such a basic form before, and on the 80,000 tea bowls and saucers, because there were so many of them. In the event the primeval appeal of gold, and the fact it was in shapes that had never previously appeared on the market, worked wonders. (In fact, most of the bids for the gold were well below the first extravagant £53,297.) The tea bowls were disposed of through the skills of Colin Sheaf, who had the crucial task of dividing the cargo up into saleable lots.

The plan was to appeal to as wide a range of bidders as possible. So the tea bowls were on offer in lots of a thousand – and in lots of half a dozen. Dealers snapped up the large lots; individuals the small. The better quality porcelain was assembled into vast dinner services in the expectation that it might attract the attention of embassies, large corporations, department stores and hotels. (Christie's ensured that such institutions were aware of the auction through direct mail shots.) The biggest service comprised one hundred and forty-four place settings, although lots with seventy-two place settings were also available. Fortunately, the most common design of the tableware being transported by the *Geldermalsen* was what is known as "Lattice Fence", which appeals as much to modern taste as it obviously did to mid-eighteenth century buyers. The bulk of the services were composed of pieces of "Lattice Fence" decoration, and they sold very well. Indeed, one of the few regrets that Colin Sheaf had after the sale was that he did not put together more large services.

In the event the demand was so great that the ordinary people, whose imagination was caught by Hatcher's adventure and who put in bids close to the catalogue estimates, were disappointed. However many of the dealers, cashing in on the publicity, were offering items immediately after the sale at still reasonable prices. They were not confident that the Hatcher appeal would last for long.

What had set the seal on the success of the auction was the confirmation that the ship discovered *was* the *Geldermalsen*. The information had been held back to create a second burst of publicity in March. All the evidence from the cargo had pointed to it being this vessel, lost in 1752, but not until the ship's bell was recovered, along with two bronze cannon (one later bought by Max de Rham) in a special second dive in early 1986 was Dr Christiaan Jorg of Groningen, the expert on Dutch trade with the Indies, able to go ahead and publish a book on the whole adventure, which made a timely arrival just before the auction to confer historical respectability on the salvage operation.

Dr Jorg's book told the dramatic story of the loss of the *Geldermalsen* pieced together from the evidence of the survivors. What had been a volume of mid-eighteenth century porcelain lost at sea for centuries was now a tale flushed out with real characters. The objects stretched across time to appeal to a later generation. In particular, the Dutch were determined to welcome home this long-delayed cargo and almost 20,000 people queued, often for over two hours, often in the rain, outside Christie's Amsterdam offices on the pre-sale viewing days to be allowed a brief glimpse of the porcelain, laid out in row upon dazzling row. They were kept warm with free coffee from the Hilton.

In 1752 the cargo of the *Geldermalsen* on arrival in the Netherlands would have been divided up by wholesalers on the quay and sent off to the "India shops" run by "China-men" where the public would buy. In 1986 anyone could turn up at the auction and make a bid. At one time the 5,000 "bidding" paddles seemed in danger of running out, but disaster was just averted.

The auctioneers discreetly sweated; the seven telephones manned alongside the rostrum rang constantly with bids from far away; attention never wavered. Occasionally a lot had to be re-bid, but considering the hundreds of first-time buyers the hesitancies were few. A representative item from each lot was displayed on a revolve to remind potential buyers just what they were in for. It all went quickly, professionally, undramatically, inexorably. All the time, two young Christie's staff cycled the few hundred yards from the Hilton to Christie's offices with the prices. Within the first hour Christie's, and Hatcher, knew that their concerted marketing operation had succeeded. The *Geldermalsen* had come home.

6

Nanking for All

Where is the Nanking cargo now? It is scattered around the world. The most expensive lot from the auction, the dinner service which made the record breaking price of almost £220,000, is in Switzerland. The new owner, who comes originally from the Middle East, secured three hundred and eighty pieces for his money, put together into a service by Christie's. If he smashes a few it hardly matters: he bought three more services at the sale.

At the other extreme there are many thousands of owners of just one piece of the cargo, usually a tea bowl and saucer, which made up half the total haul. It may well be the only antique that they have in their home and they acquired it not out of any great love of, or interest in, Chinese eighteenth-century porcelain but because their imaginations had been gripped by Hatch's adventurous expedition.

That the sale proved a tremendous success surprised few people, except for some of the leading dealers in Chinese works of art who,

Five little boys in blue – made around 1750 and sought after by collectors (left). *A gathering of Immortals* (above).

from their exalted position, could not believe that there would be sufficient buyers for what they considered to be a vast quantity of rather mediocre eighteenth-century export porcelain. Hatch was certain that ordinary people would respond to his achievement, but he played along with Christie's strategy of placing very low estimates on the porcelain to encourage bids. This approach, coupled with the vast amount of publicity, brought in the enquiries and stimulated the interest. A total of around £7 million was perhaps the best inside estimate for the sale, double the official forecast. The £10 million topped most peoples' expectations.

But not those of David Howard, of Mayfair dealers Heirloom and Howard. He had been a supporter of Hatch right from the beginning, buying heavily at the Ming sale. He had come to antique dealing after a career in marketing and, with a love of history, is as interested in the origins of ceramics as in their aesthetic beauty. The Nanking cargo was a natural for him, and he was the biggest individual buyer at the sale, spending £600,000 at the auction and another £350,000 immediately after the sale.

"I told all our clients that prices would be three or four times the estimates", he says. Some took his advice and raised their bids; others stuck to Christie's estimates and missed out. In the event Howard, who attended the auction loaded with bids commissioned by clients, was also keen to acquire porcelain on his own account. Those of his regular clients whose bids failed to match the saleroom price levels were offered pieces that Howard had bought at the auction price, plus a modest ten per cent premium. Hence the need for the dealer to try and acquire as many items as possible from fellow dealers after the auction, to build up his depleted stocks.

There was, in effect, a second auction of the Nanking cargo in the hotel rooms of Amsterdam and down the international telephone lines during, and immediately after, the auction at the Hilton. Very few of today's owners of Nanking porcelain actually secured their treasure at Christie's, or at the prices ruling there. Dealers traded with dealers, with large department stores, with hotels and restaurants, with companies, and with some important private collectors, who realized late in the day that they were missing out on one of the great saleroom phenomena of our time. Suddenly everyone wanted the Nanking.

For Colin Sheaf, one of the auctioneers, it was a joy to conduct a sale in which familiar faces jostled with thousands of the unknown. As well as David Howard, other leading London dealers such as Marchant and Cohen and Pearce were in their seats on all five days. So were all the major continental dealers in Chinese export porcelain – Bernheimer, Perrotto and Myers. Perhaps more pleasing, there was an important American museum buying study examples, as well as American business syndicates who had pooled resources to buy large lots of dishes. The Ritz Hotel was there, and tea companies anxious to acquire tea bowls and saucers for promotional purposes. And an undisclosed Royal Family (perhaps Dutch) and pop stars (perhaps Elton John).

Ironically, the items that seemed to pose the biggest problem – the tea bowls and saucers – have proved the greatest success since the sale. Compared to the other lots they were (relative) bargains and, because they could be offered to the public at affordable prices, they have become the touchstone of the Nanking cargo. The experiences of David Howard would be typical for a dealer. With the addition of Christie's buyer's premium and local taxes he was paying around £40 at auction for a tea bowl and saucer. He was offering it in his shop at around £70, adding on his usual commission. At this price it was within the budget of the man in the street – and so it proved.

He has never been so busy as in the month after the Amsterdam sale. A taxi driver, putting down a passenger outside Heirloom & Howards Grafton Street shop, emptied the cash from his box and

A collection of "Nanking" at Heirloom & Howard.

bought a piece of the Nanking. Christie's, which was flooded with enquiries, was referring eager buyers to the dealers it knew had bought at auction, and would-be purchasers dashed around London from dealer to dealer, worried that they might be too late to get their memento.

It became socially competitive. Howard tells of receiving an order from a certain house in a certain street in a certain London suburb. He was able to supply a tea bowl and saucer. A week later he received a similar request from the house next door. Then more, from houses down the street. In the end he had despatched twenty-one items of Nanking to just that one quiet suburban road.

But when prices moved above £100 Nanking items became harder to sell to those simply gripped by the glamour of its recovery. Dealers who were known to have bought tea bowls and saucers by the thousand were approached by businessmen, who saw their way to a quick fortune. Soon advertisements were appearing in the newspapers

offering a piece of the Nanking at £180. They found some buyers but anyone who secured a bowl and cup at this price, with the mark up of perhaps two dealers on top of the auction price, will own a piece of history rather than a readily cashable investment. By the end of 1986 a more reasonable price for a bowl and saucer would be nearer £120. But very few are on offer. Most owners are proud and pleased with their purchase and have no wish to sell.

The shrewdest dealers sold out most of their stock in the month after the auction when the publicity was at its greatest. A lengthy documentary on BBC Television, using John Bremmer's film of the actual salvaging operation and following through to the success of the auction, provided thousands of pounds worth of free publicity and sustained the enthusiasm. Newspapers recognized a good story, and offered Nanking blue and white as prizes in circulation-boosting competitions.

For most dealers, their main customers were those of their fellow dealers who had been wrong-footed by the appeal of the auction, and wholesalers. But often these late-comers have paid for their caution. With almost 80,000 tea bowls and saucers on offer, anyone who really wanted a set could acquire one relatively cheaply after the auction. When the later dealers had added on another mark-up, pushing prices up to unreasonable levels, they came across customer resistance. Any dealer hanging on to a bowl and saucer for six months after the sale would have been holding a depreciating antique. And any collector who

A mother suckling her baby, a lady, a dignitary (with child) and two ponies (left).

"Nanking" for sale in Harrods of London (right).

jumped late on to the bandwagon will have to wait for Hatch to discover another wreck before prices reach again the peak of the summer of 1986.

Many members of the public have acquired their "Hatcher" not direct from their local antique shop, or a dealer, but from one of the major department stores. Harrods quickly appreciated the appeal of the Nanking and sent one of its buyers to the sale. Unfortunately, the prices exceeded his budget and he returned empty-handed. But so strong was the public interest that Harrods decided to acquire some anyway, from dealers, and from a Norwegian middle-man, who had bought heavily at the sale purely as an investment. By June 7 it had some on offer and in the late summer, in its capacious central hall, Harrods created a mock-up of the wreck, the *Geldermalsen*'s ribs showing above the sand, and with nets and barnacles completing the underwater tableau. It proved a great success, with first day crowds reminiscent of a Harrods sale. Many came to gaze, but there were enough buyers for Harrods to maintain the promotion for months. Prices ranged from £75 for a chocolate cup to £75,000 for one of the large fish dishes – six times its price at auction, suggesting some lucrative profit-taking on its way to Knightsbridge. In all Harrods sold well over 1,000 pieces. Liberty's was another London store that went nap on Hatch, and at both you can still buy a plate or two, although now there is little available at under £1,000 an item.

In contrast Harrods' New York rival Bloomingdales was much less successful with its Nanking promotion. It bought itself into the act late but by making the rounds of the dealers secured a reasonable display, often, like Harrods, taking it on a sale or return basis. It even persuaded Hatch to go to New York to give some sparkle to the opening. But its

Bloomingdales in New York had its own sale of "Hatcher".

publicity department failed to make much of the occasion and little of the porcelain sold – perhaps because Bloomingdales had added very high profit margins. Pieces were on offer at five times the price that they could be bought in London.

It is a curious aspect of the whole business that the only country yet to be touched by the Hatcher saga is the US. Relatively few American buyers came to Amsterdam – although the second largest dinner service went to a wealthy American for £172,000 – and the American media has been unmoved by his story. Perhaps it is because the wreck was found so far from its shores; perhaps because the US has enough treasure wrecks of its own to be hunted off its coasts, in particular around Florida; perhaps it is because Americans remain insular and are only really interested in the deeds of fellow Americans: whatever the reason Hatch has still to storm the US. There was, however, one pleasing exception: that southern tourist attraction, Colonial Williamsburg, appreciated that the porcelain was exactly the right period for its eighteenth-century mansions and bought a stack.

The Nanking may not be flashy enough for American taste — there were after all, enthusiastic Texan millionaires buying the more dramatic blue and white porcelain from the Ming cargo — but it certainly appeals to the Europeans. The UK took more of the Nanking than any other single country, but there were determined buyers from Germany, France, Switzerland and Scandinavia. Significantly, it was not to the liking of the rich Hong Kong, Taiwan and Singapore buyers of Chinese porcelain: they prefer the top quality Imperial Ming pieces. The *Geldermalsen* cargo was originally designed for export to Europe and that is where it eventually ended up.

It is ironic that — while the unappreciated tea bowls and saucers, which the divers could hardly be bothered to pack at the end of the salvaging, have become the most popular items for sale — the pieces which have proved hardest to dispose of have been the private cargo goods, the Immortals, horses, etc, carried by the ship's officers as presents, or for private gain.

They were sold at the very end of the auction when buyers were carried away by the constant high prices and the desperation to get hold of something. While David Howard had sold by the end of 1986 almost ninety-nine per cent of the routine Nanking porcelain, he still had available fifteen out of the fifty private cargo pieces he bought. He paid £1,300 for one of the small smiling boys wearing only a blue shirt; he would probably now accept £1,300 for it. All the publicity has done nothing to shake the belief of serious collectors of Chinese porcelain, the traditional customer for such unique items, that the Nanking cargo contains nothing of the quality they look for in their purchases. Its mass appeal has deterred the connoisseurs — perhaps it is their loss.

Dealers who invested £40,000 in a thousand tea bowls and saucers probably sold them for £100,000. But this is hardly trading in antiques. On the other hand, the more erudite dealer who, appreciating the design of the big fish dishes, paid £20,000 for one would have a hard task finding a buyer at £40,000. His best hope would have been to be bidding at the auction on behalf of a committed collector. The vomit cups did well because of their curiosity value — they appealed to traditional buyers who had never seen one before and to the rich first-time purchaser. On the other hand, the twelve-inch saucer dishes

Hatch can eat off his find at the Ritz in London.

have sold less well, mainly because they do not have an immediate practical use in the contemporary home.

There is no reason why much of the Nanking cargo should not be used in daily life: not perhaps constantly but to set off special occasions. Even the items which are completely out of fashion, such as the vomit cups, make excellent soup bowls. The porcelain was designed to be used by the European middle class of the eighteenth century: it is appropriate that their successors should be enjoying it.

In fact anyone can eat off Nanking cargo porcelain – by dining at the Ritz. The hotel was a successful bidder in Amsterdam and has furnished its Trafalgar Suite with a twenty-place service from the wreck. It is proving a good investment, for the Ritz charges each guest a £10 premium for the experience, on top of its regular price. So great is the demand for the service that the hotel should soon recoup its £30,000 investment at the auction.

A third great British institution, along with Harrods and the Ritz, appreciated the importance, and the popular appeal, of Hatch's find – the British Museum. It had earlier acquired some pieces from the Ming and, buying through a dealer, it added over thirty pieces of Nanking. Unlike many dealers, the British Museum is buying for posterity. It is well aware of the importance of the Nanking cargo in the history of Chinese works of art and the interest it will have for scholars in a hundred years' time.

One of the most far-reaching consequences of the discovery, and the successful marketing, of the cargo from the *Geldermalsen* has been the boost it has given to the collection of Chinese porcelain. Most owners of a piece of the Nanking will be content with that single item; but some, and they could number into the thousands, have discovered the joys of collecting. David Howard can point to a filing cabinet with the names of a thousand new customers who came to him through the purchase of a Nanking bowl or plate. He now mails them all. Perhaps they cannot afford to pay more than £100 at the moment, but they may well become knowledgeable and hooked – and richer.

Already a new breed of collector has appeared: one who buys objects recovered from wrecks. Some dealers had just the thing to develop their collection – items from the Ming cargo. Indeed, while searching in vain for the *Geldermalsen*, Hatch had brought up a few more seventeenth-century blue and white Ming pieces, sometimes cracked but saleable. Not much Ming was left unsold by 1986 but anything available in a reasonable condition, sold well on the back of Nanking.

It is a good thing that the Nanking created its own band of new collectors because most of the traditional buyers of eighteenth-century Chinese export porcelain sat on their hands at the sale. This reluctance to purchase was less true of some of the unusual and costly items, such as the fish dishes, and some serious collectors also wanted a memento of the occasion, but, in the main, the Nanking has established its own quite separate market, away from the mainstream of Chinese porcelain. If anything it has given a slight boost to overall prices in what was quite a strong market anyway, but at the Chinese ceramics auctions of Sotheby's and Christie's, and in the shops of the main dealers in London, Paris and New York, there has been little apparent change in price levels. Somehow 160,000 extra pieces, equal to around five years normal supply, have been absorbed.

Christie's is currently reluctant to accept for re-sale items from the Nanking. It feels it is too soon. The filtration process is not yet complete. In a year or so Nanking will be bought and sold at prices higher than equivalent objects without its special provenance, but to different buyers, and according to different criteria. Its romantic origin will always be its main attraction, not the actual quality of the plate or pot.

It was wise of Christie's to mark every item it sold with a distinctive Nanking mark. This will prevent similar export porcelain sailing under false "Hatcher" credentials. There is a slight danger of forgeries, but at the moment prices do not encourage such a risky business, and, with the lavishly illustrated catalogue, any forgeries would be quickly uncovered.

The gold ingots appealed to at least three types of rich buyers – the collector of jewels and precious metals; the speculator in gold; and the committed connoisseur of Chinese works of art, anxious to add to his collection one of the eighteen bars shaped like a shoe which had been unknown before Hatch. Prices followed the pattern of all the sections at the auction – very high at the start; then a fall; and a rise near the end as supplies dwindled. A private European collector must feel he has paid over the odds – £53,000, twenty times its bullion value – for the first gold ingot offered; the remainder of the shoe-shaped pieces fall into the £20,000-£23,000 category. Because of their rarity, and their intrinsic value, they are likely to appreciate nicely in price.

The conventional gold bars were less sought-after but they still attracted serious buyers of Chinese treasures. Bluett, the London dealer, which sat out most of the sessions because the material was not distinctive enough for its erudite clients, paid £15,000 for one of the gold bars; most of the remainder went modestly for around £5,000 each, only three times their bullion value. This shows what the real demand is for rare Chinese works of art – there are only a few hundred rich collectors in the world, and by offering one hundred and twenty-five bars Christie's exhausted those interested.

Perhaps the nicest thing about the Nanking cargo is the variety of its appeal, and the wide range of its new owners. There was no trouble at all in selling the made-up dinner services – Christie's would have raised extra money if it had assembled more such groups – and now a fortunate lunch guest at a boardroom table in the City of London, or in New York, may be surrounded by gleaming Nanking as he eats. Dealers who acquired sufficient pieces have composed their own services to sell to the rich, who get a boost from owning and using crockery with such a romantic story.

Most of the 160,000 items of Nanking porcelain are in secure homes. The dealers have been cleaned out but retailers like to offer it, gift-wrapped and with a certificate of authenticity, to tempt customers looking for a special anniversary or wedding present. They will have to pay dearly for their prize. The more flamboyant porcelain – the fish dishes, the vomit cups, the private cargo statues – will have joined some of the great collections of Chinese works of art, but most of the bowls and plates are the glory of private homes to be brought into use at great celebrations.

In suburban homes and in museums, in smart hotels and in corporate dining rooms, in the collections of Hatch, Mr Ong and some fellow divers, in the gift departments of fancy stores and in the carefully guarded collections of connoisseurs, the Nanking has found a much better home than the sea bed. Immediately after the Amsterdam auction, it was relatively good value; it then rose to excessive heights as middle men tried to cash in on the publicity; and it has now settled at a lower but still healthy premium. Anyone who really wants a piece of Hatch's find can have a piece. Despite the mutterings of the top dealers, it has not flooded the market for Chinese export porcelain: it has given it a slight boost. It has certainly brought in a new generation of collectors. Above all the Nanking cargo has given a great deal of pleasure to a great many people.

7

Divers' Tales

Although there are many parallels between Hatch and the freebooting sea-faring adventurers of the sixteenth and seventeenth centuries – a dislike of authority, a positive desire to take chances, a willingness to confront the elements – he is also very much a man of the future: the salvaging of underwater wrecks seems set to become one of the great quests of the next decade. While people have been besotted with outer space there is much more to learn – and to public benefit – from the sea bed. The equipment needed to explore beneath the sea is steadily becoming more sophisticated and practical (much of it spin-offs from military research). The new technology makes underwater salvaging very expensive but the potential discoveries are legion. Thousands upon thousand of ships await exploration: most will be mainly of interest to marine archaeologists; some will yield great treasures.

It is not hard to pinpoint where the wrecks are likely to be. Mariners always hugged the coastline as far as was possible. Just as on today's roads, the sea has its notorious black spots – rocks and reefs, shallows and currents – where vessels are most likely to flounder, especially in bad weather. There are many reefs like the Admiral Stellingwerf in the South China Sea, and every ocean has its danger zones. In the UK the Scilly Islands are the graveyard for thousands of vessels.

Anyone interested in underwater salvaging can easily find books listing wrecks. Of course many vessels would have been salvaged soon after they went down – luring boats on to rocks was a profitable pastime in eighteenth-century Cornwall (and in many other places). Ships that came to grief on rocks and in dangerous waters usually broke up, and today both the vessel and its cargo are long since scattered and destroyed. But there is no shortage of possibilities, albeit most of them will prove disillusioning.

Just how frustrating and risky underwater salvaging can be is described by perhaps the leading British explorer in the field, Rex Cowan, who has been a professional wreck-hunter for eighteen years (after a career as a solicitor) and who is a member of the Runciman Committee, an advisory body to the British Government on the licensing and designation of wrecks.

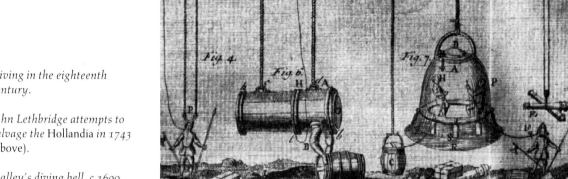

Diving in the eighteenth century.

John Lethbridge attempts to salvage the Hollandia *in 1743 (above).*

Halley's diving bell, c.1690, from an original print.

He has recently underaken an expedition to dive the wreck of the *Vliegenthart*. He has spent seven years on the search, discovery and excavation of the wreck site. A great deal of time was spent positioning his chartered vessel over the site, preparing moorings, and doing the initial archaeological work which is now virtually compulsory for salvagers. The cost of hiring a ship and equipment, devising special equipment for the dive, and the daily operational expenses produced a bill of almost £30,000. In addition there were the wages of seven divers and helpers to be found. The reward from the last year of this potentially important operation was two clay galley bricks, not much for a season's diving.

Cowan can live with such a setback because he had earlier recovered an East India Company money-chest of gold and silver coins from the

Rex Cowan (left) *dividing gold coins from the* Vliegenthart *with officials from the Dutch Government.*

A wooden gun carriage wheel from the ship encrusted with gold and silver coins.

A sister ship of the Vliegenthart (right).

wreck site, which he is carefully selling on the market. Perhaps the great difference between Hatch and most of his rivals in the field is that Hatch is luckier in finding the wrecks. Even so he had two fruitless voyages before he found the *"G"* – and he was quite prepared to mount another expedition when the 1985 enterprise looked like ending in stalemate.

Although most ships go down in relatively shallow water near the coasts, time and the weather can shift the wrecks into deeper water. It is only in recent years, with the development of diving bells and midget submarines, that men have been able to salvage at more than one hundred and fifty feet. Not that all the great potential finds are in the deep waters.

One of the pains and pleasures of the search is that the underwater geography can change daily. Sydney Wignall, another British diver, recalls the day when he was diving the *Royal Charter*, one of the most famous wrecks in British waters. The clipper was driven on to the Anglesey rocks in 1859 on its way to Liverpool from the Australian gold fields. It was heavy with gold and, while much was discovered immediately after the disaster, treasure is still to be found near the carefully signposted spot where the ship was lost.

As Wignall discovered: in 1958 he came across a bar of gold bullion. Unfortunately he was out of air when he found the gold. He returned to the surface determined to re-dive the area when he could lay his hands on more oxygen. But in the meantime a storm had blown up and when he got back underwater the configuration of the wreck had changed completely. A bar of gold, worth around £400,000, lies in fifteen feet of water just twenty yards out from the rocks. There are perhaps five million scuba divers in the US and Europe alone and most of them hope one day to have Wignall's experience – with a happier ending.

One of the problems about underwater salvaging is that the law on ownership is so confused, differs from country to country, and opens such a legal minefield, that many divers keep quiet about any lucrative finds they make. Fishermen, especially in the Mediterranean, have long supplemented their earnings with coins, statues and pots that they have found in the waters around Italy, Greece and Turkey. A German museum recently paid £500,000 for a statue recovered off the coast of Sicily. Its gain is Italy's loss, but many keen antique collectors, as well as museums, only have eyes for the objects they are offered, not their provenance.

Most of the most famous wrecks of history have defied the salvagers. The *Titanic* is the classic example – but for how much longer, now that it has been photographed on the ocean floor? Often the most rewarding wrecks are completely unknown – such as the junk carrying the Ming porcelain recovered by Hatch: the Chinese shipping records for the period no longer exist. Hatch has his own list of potential wrecks, which he keeps close to his chest, but just some of the vessels that have gone down in Indonesian waters in which he is interested are the *Lendenhof*, another Dutch East Indiaman which came to grief in 1765; the *Ontario*, an American vessel lost in the nineteenth century; and the *Franfort*, a British ship which sank in 1862.

East Indiamen, British, Dutch and Portuguese, are particularly interesting because, on their homeward journey, they were loaded with merchandise. But often on their voyage to the east they were carrying gold or silver bullion. They are among the great prizes for today's salvagers and they are being discovered with surprising frequency. Only six months after Christie's Amsterdam offered the Nanking cargo, it held an auction of five hundred and forty-two silver bars recovered from the *Bredenhof*, a VOC vessel which, like the *Geldermalsen*, was owned by the Zeeland chamber. It had actually been built in the same year, 1746, as the "G".

The *Bredenhof* was on its way to Bengal with a cargo of gold and silver, the silver to be minted into rupees. It sunk on June 6, 1753 in the treacherous Mozambique channel, just eighteen months after the *Geldermalsen*. Its loss was a grievous blow to the Zeeland chamber because in 1752, as well as the *Geldermalsen*, another of its East Indiamen, the *Wapen van Hoorn*, also failed to come home.

Like the "G" the *Bredenhof* hit a reef in calm water, thirteen miles off the African coast. As it slowly broke up, the captain ordered that the silver, in fourteen chests, should be dropped overboard to lighten the load and to prevent plundering by the crew. He hid the gold ducats on his person as he made for shore on a makeshift raft. Around two hundred of the crew managed to reach an African landfall but less than half this number survived the one hundred and twenty mile trek to the Portuguese settlement then known as Mocambique. The spot where the silver had been off-loaded was not marked by buoys because the chests lay in only three fathoms of water and could easily be seen from the surface. In 1754 an attempt was made by the authorities in the Netherlands to recover the silver but it seemed to have disappeared: had the Portuguese got there first? A second salvaging expedition the next year ended equally fruitlessly, with recrimination between Dutch, Portuguese and native fishermen.

The loss of the *Bredenhof* was meticulously recorded in the Dutch archives and there are plenty of clues to its resting place. The main question was whether any of the silver still remained on the sea bed. A Cayman's Island company contracted with Captain Ernst Klaar to undertake a salvaging operation and in the oriental junk, the *Maria José*, he set out on May 29, 1986. His experiences make familiar reading. No luck at the first location; then a storm, which threw the crew into the sea and threatened to destroy their magnetometer; then success with the "fish", and the discovery – of just one bar of silver, all on its own.

Although plagued by dirty water and the same strong currents that brought low the VOC vessel, Klaar's team began to find silver in very varying condition – by the time of the auction he could offer two hundred and forty-one bars in almost mint condition, with fine VOC markings; one hundred and twenty-four bars with marks, but affected by the sea; and another one hundred and eighty odd bars which had lost their markings and had sometimes fused together, making them works of "sea sculpture." It seems as if some of the cargo had drifted, over the years, fifteen miles from the site of the actual wreck. This was the largest quantity of eighteenth century Dutch silver bars to be offered at auction and it made £138,000.

The total was only a third higher than the bullion value of the silver, and drives home the point that the millions made from the Nanking cargo were very much the exception. Most wrecks are expensive to salvage and often, even when saleable objects are retrieved, they fail to recoup the costs of the expedition. The *Bredenhof* was one of the best known, and most sought after, wrecks on the treasure hunters lists, and yet the recovery of its long lost cargo has made no-one's fortune.

Perhaps the most encouraging feature of the auction was the presence of London dealers, who are starting to appreciate the marketing appeal of art from the sea bed. The dealer Baldwin paid £4,600 for eight bars of silver, fused together over the centuries; he had to compete against Vandekar and other London dealers.

The roll-call of the East Indiamen, both Dutch and British, that failed to make it to port is long and doleful – the *Middleburg*, the *Haarlem*, the *Merestijn*, the *Grosvenor*, the *Prince of Wales*, and many more. One of the most intriguing is the *Dodington* which, in 1754, in squally weather, hit the uncharted Bird Island, off the eastern coast of South Africa. It was carrying gold and silver, the property of Clive of India who was travelling on another ship in the flotilla.

In 1977 two South African scuba divers, David Allen and Gerry van Niekerk went looking for the *Dodington*. They had done their researches well in the archives and found the wreck on their first dive. They have since recovered silver coins, copper ingots, and personal items such as pipes and scissors but no gold. Perhaps the surviving members of the crew made off with it, perhaps burying it on the African coast? As Hatch says, "When a ship started to break up in those days all hell broke loose: the crew got drunk, killed their officers, and fought over the gold." The evidence of survivors at subsequent courts of enquiry might look like impressive and factual testimony, but a great deal of treasure was lost to crew members or was scattered in the confusion.

In all, it is estimated that over two hundred ships of the English East India Company were lost in the two centuries after 1600, and the Dutch had proportionate disasters. Many of the ships have just disappeared without trace. The *Cabalava* set off for China from the UK in 1818 with £200,000 in silver coins among her cargo. She was lost on a reef between Mauritius and the Seychelles and still awaits a salvager. Some vessels have no known resting place, such as the *Skelton Castle*, last seen rounding the Cape of Good Hope in 1806, hot foot for Madras. A wonderful find would be the *Prince of Wales*, also lost off the Cape, in 1804, the flagship of a convoy homeward-bound from India and laden with treasure: she is in deep water, with no exact location, and, with current technology, is not worth a search.

Many vessels, both English and Dutch, went down in the Channel, and in particular around the Scilly Isles. One of the most famous was the *Hollandia*, a VOC ship with much silver on board. She sank in

This squashed and unidentifiable lump of copper after cleaning and restoration was revealed as the Hollandia's *ships lantern.*

Part of the treasure trove from the Hollandia *– Mexican Pillar dollars after cleaning (right).*

1743 but it was not until 1970 that the first serious attempt was made to salvage her wealth. This was Rex Cowan's first venture into diving, and, armed with authority from the Dutch Government and, for the first time in European waters, a magnetometer, he struck lucky at the end of his second season.

First, Cowan found an anchor and cannon. Then a few days later, perhaps the most wonderful discovery in his career – a mound of solid silver three feet high and thirteen feet broad: all the coins had congealed into one mass. It took many years to raise the silver from the *Hollandia* but it made Cowan's reputation and provided him with a modest cache to finance more, sometimes less lucrative, ventures.

Other Dutch East Indiamen to surface (at least to divers) in recent years have been the *Akerenda*, which had hit the Norwegian coast, and the *De Liefde* which, in 1711, preferred to avoid the perils of the Scillies by travelling round the British Isles, which was a foolish diversion as the ship sunk off the Skerries. Over the years some of its 200,000 silver coins have been washed onto local beaches but only in 1965 was it systematically salvaged by Scientific Survey and Location Limited and Static Devices, and since then many coins have been recovered, including 4,000 in a chest in mint condition.

The Scillies again offered up another VOC vessel in 1973 when the *Princesse Maria* was located by Rex Cowan's team. Like so many other vessels, it had been picked over during the centuries – among the scavengers was King James II who in 1686 managed to walk off with 13,000 coins during the period between when the ship hit the Western Rocks and when it sank. But even so there was still pewter, coins, and some navigational equipment awaiting today's searchers.

An East Indiaman of the seventeenth century wrecked at sea.

A diver, working on the Princesse Maria, finds a candlestick.

The Amsterdam *comes into view off Hastings.*

Finds from the wreck undergo examination.

For non-divers, the search for these East Indiamen might well seem exciting, but rather exclusive. They can join in the rescue operation through the films taken by John Bremmer and others, but the actual look of an eighteenth-century merchantman, in its final resting place, would seem to be outside their experience. But it need not be. By a freak of nature only three years before the "G" was lost in the South China Sea a very similar vessel, the *Amsterdam*, ended its life in Hastings, of all places. And at low tide it can still be seen, lying quietly on the sand, much of its structure intact. There are moves afoot to transport the *Amsterdam* back to its home port, funds willing. Most years, there are carefully controlled investigations of the wreck by historians, and although most of its cargo was rescued soon after it sank, with periodic ventures from looters in the intervening years when weather changes exposed the wreck more than usual, there are still to be found on the site many personal artifacts. It is the best example of an old wreck for land-locked observers.

If the *Amsterdam* gives an excellent impression of the size and appearance of the *Geldermalsen*, the "G"'s cargo mirrors that of the *Göteborg* which sank, appropriately enough, in the harbour at Gothenberg in 1745 and was scientifically salvaged by the Swedes in 1905. The "G" is not the first East Indiamen to offer up its merchandise after centuries on the sea bed, but it is nevertheless unparalleled in the size and the condition of what Hatch and his team managed to salvage. For all the criticism of archaeologists, the "G" was the most comprehensive find of its type ever, a true landmark in underwater recovery.

Most divers are able, through modern technological breakthroughs, to make a thorough investigation of known wrecks, but rarely do they work a virgin site. Also sea water has destroyed many of the old cargoes – in particular textiles, spices and base metals. On the "G", the tea was lost, but the porcelain was pristine. Hatch has set himself an almost impossible task as he looks for his next prey. It is unlikely to be another East Indiamen: they have either been picked over or are in impossibly deep, or unknown waters.

Hatch has just one rival as an under-sea treasure hunter – the American Mel Fisher. Fortunately Fisher concentrates on the waters around Florida. Although Hatch is now looking for a broader canvas than the South China Sea, and has the time, money and expertise to hunt wrecks anywhere in the world and at unprecedented depths, he is not attracted to the Caribbean and the US coastal strip. That is Fisher's territory. In turn he leaves the orient to Hatch.

By chance Fisher made his great discovery only a couple of months after Hatch located the *Geldermalsen*. His had been a long and costly search, taking sixteen years and eating up around $10 million. In the end his endurance was rewarded with a treasure that matches that of Hatch – the gold bullion and silver ingots of a Spanish galleon, the *Nuestra Senora de Atocha*, which was sunk by a hurricane off the Florida Keys in 1622.

The *Atocha* was well worth the effort. It was carrying part of the annual treasure tribute from the Spanish colonies to their royal master in Madrid and the current value of its cargo has been estimated at $180 million. For long it had been at the top of every serious diver's hit list of desirable finds. Indeed in 1688 the Spanish authorities were still hunting it: an attempt to recover the gold and silver immediately after the ship went down was foiled by the depth of water – fifty-five feet, a major obstacle in the 1620s but a lovely diving depth today.

The search for the *Atocha* has striking parallels with Hatch's endeavours. Quick initial success – then long disappointment; trouble with the authorities; misinformation about the siting of the wreck; interference from rival divers – and finally, when hope was running out, the bonanza. But Fisher's ups and downs spread over years rather than months. Together, the two case histories provide invaluable knowledge to any future treasure seekers.

It was the publication in 1960 of John S. Potter Jnr's *The Treasure Divers Guide*, which listed the most appetizing wrecks off the Florida coast, linked to the development of more sophisticated diving equipment, that sparked off the chase for the *Atocha*. Fisher, like Hatch, had had an earlier, very profitable, success – the salvaging of the 1715 and 1733 Spanish treasure fleets which had also fallen foul of the storms off the Florida coast. With the money made from these wrecks, he, like many other local hunters, concentrated on the *Atocha*.

He first began to look a hundred miles away from the correct location – once again the wrong conclusions had been drawn from the historical records. The Matecumbe Keys, where the contemporary sources said that *Atocha* had hit the rocks, had been re-named in subsequent years. The searchers were looking in the wrong place. Even when the right islands had been pinpointed, a loose translation from the Archives of the Indies, which are kept in Seville, had Fisher prospecting on the east side when he should have been on the west. These delays were proving costly and Fisher had already spent $250,000.

Unlike Hatch, who funds all his expeditions personally, with a similar commitment from his partners in United Subsea Services, Fisher pays for his treasure-seeking mainly by attracting investments from the public on the promise of a share of the loot. It is an approach that breeds problems. To persuade investors to stump up, Fisher is under pressure to produce good evidence for eventual success. When he found the anchor of a galleon it was very much in his interest to convince the world that it was an anchor from the *Atocha*.

But the Government of Florida, already suspicious about the activities of so many freebooting explorers rummaging in its coastal waters, was critical of what looked like a way of detaching people from their money on flimsy evidence. As early as 1967 Florida had placed all wrecks in state waters under its jurisdiction, permitting salvaging only after a specific contract for a site had been agreed, with Florida receiving twenty-five per cent of the value of any funds. These bureaucratic tentacles would not have suited Hatch and they gave Fisher many expensive nightmares.

Gold and silver ware from the Atocha, with a concentrated lump of pieces of eight and other treasures (left).

A gold medallion found in late 1986 (above).

The months dragged into years. Objects were recovered – coins, silver ingots, even a gold bar – but nothing to convince the authorities that Fisher had discovered the *Atocha*. The finds were scattered on the sea bed. The main cargo – the "motherload" – remained elusive. In an attempt to persuade Florida, both its Government and its potential investors, that he was on the right track Fisher hired an archaeologist, R. Duncan Mathewson III, to help provide conclusive proof and to assist in the location of the wreck.

As in the arguments over the *Geldermalsen*, the historians want very convincing evidence before relics from the sea bed can actually be attributed to a particular vessel. Hatch had to go back and re-dive the *Geldermalsen* finally to persuade Christie's and the Dutch Government that he had the "G." Fisher, even when he produced silver ingots carrying markings known to be on the *Atocha*'s manifest, was unable to get an official confirmation – the ingots could have been transferred to another vessel; the Spanish might have used the same markings a hundred years later. On the basis of coins, swords (the *Atocha* was well armed), and pottery (including fragments of Chinese blue and white) Mathewson was convinced Fisher had the *Atocha*. But much was missing – cannon, anchors, the actual main hull of the ship.

In a striking parallel to the hunt for the *Geldermalsen*, Fisher became convinced that the main cargo, and the bulk of the ship, had hit the bottom some way away from his initial discoveries. Like Hatch he embarked on a long, slow, costly search in ever widening circles. But while Hatch had to work in weeks, Fisher's quest took years. The morale of his crew of young American divers began to sag and he kept up spirits by telling them every morning, "Todays the day"; he even had sweat shirts printed with the message.

But today was rarely the day. In 1975 his son Dirk found five cannon. One of them carried a number which matched the records in Seville. Surely this was proof positive? But, before the team could celebrate, tragedy hit. One of the yachts suddenly capsized in the night drowning Dirk Fisher, his wife and another crew member. Mel Fisher had paid a dreadful price in his obsession to find the *Atocha*. By now, the value of its cargo was almost secondary to the need to prove that all his time, all the money, and the lives of his dear ones had not been thrown away.

For another decade Fisher returned each spring to the Florida Keys to continue the hunt for the elusive "motherload." He used magnetometer, sub-bottom sonar and aerial photography to draw up maps of the sea bed. Always there were enough tantalizing finds to motivate the divers when despair set in, and finally, in 1980, they hit upon the hull of a ship. It turned out to be the *Margarita*, a sister ship to the *Atocha*, and also loaded with treasure, but one which had been salvaged by the Spaniards immediately after the disaster. Even so forty-three gold chains were recovered and Fisher's investors had a much needed gush of confidence in him.

The magnetometer had been trawled over the spot on many occasions and showed up nothing. It took a series of storms to clear away the sand and reveal the hull to the divers: there is no safe alternative to the human eye and hand. With the money to be made from the gold and silver recovered from the *Margarita*, Fisher could continue the search for the *Atocha*.

Finally, almost to the day when Hatch and Max found the *Geldermalsen*, divers from the one hundred and sixty-seven-foot salvage vessel *Saba Rock* discovered – ballast. It was what they had been looking for for years – evidence for the stern of the *Atocha*. Close by were the gold bars, silver coins, emeralds and pieces of jewellery which made this potentially the richest underwater treasure in decades. After so many false alarms Fisher was reluctant to blow the trumpet but the weight of the evidence, over 1,040 silver ingots, one hundred and fifteen gold bars, over sixty gold and 100,000 silver coins, more than three hundred and fifty uncut emeralds, and many silver objects, convinced him that his quest was at an end.

Not that work on the *Atocha* will continue for many more years. The marine archaeologists have taken over, and expect to extract 300,000 artifacts from the site. It was good public relations for Fisher to put an historian on the payroll, but both in his suggestions on where to look for the wreck, and in the careful and controlled recovery of the treasure, which went hand in hand with a scientific survey of the remains of the ship, Mathewson has earned his keep many times over.

Times had changed radically in the fifteen years it took to find the *Atocha*. The day of the buccaneer, oblivious to legal, political and historical interests, is over. No treasure hunter, at least no treasure hunter operating in territorial waters, can afford to ignore public and Governmental opinion. Fisher learned this the hard way, but by playing along he has been able to enjoy most of his find.

The actual return on the *Atocha* is hard to calculate. The cost of the excavation was immense – not only the cost of hiring equipment, food and fuel, payment of professional advisers – but the inevitable legal costs as Government, suppliers and competitors infringed on the operations. Fisher took advantage of the new wave of salvage companies, set up by entrepreneurs, which sell a stake of any treasure found to investors. It is not hard to promote such companies: many people would be prepared to risk some of their savings in such an adventure. In many cases all will be lost, but if the leader of the expedition does make a successful hit the rewards can be tremendous.

Treasure Salvors Inc, Fisher's company, paid out to over 1,100 investors in November 1986. They were not paid in cash, rather in kind, each receiving Spanish gold coins to the value of $18,000 for each $1,000 invested. They have the problem of disposing of them on the market, a tricky proposition with so much gold and silver becoming suddenly available.

Although the treasure cargo of the *Atocha* and the *Margarita* sounds more glamorous than Hatch's blue and white plates and pots, in saleable terms Hatch made the better find. There is a limit to the number of collectors for old gold and silver coins, while the Nanking porcelain has a practical and decorative attraction. The *Atocha* gold should do well, but the silver may take years to distribute. Much will depend on the promotional campaign launched in the US. Undoubtedly Fisher's find, just when Hatch was preparing for the Amsterdam auction, took away some of his glory.

The divers working for Fisher were rewarded according to their length of service. Around a dozen of them are believed to be in line for one per cent of the estimated value while the rest could receive anything between $150,000 and $250,000. The Florida wrecks will be prospected for more seasons, probably yielding rich but diminishing returns. It was a great salvage operation but in its financial complexity, its merchandizing and PR back up, its time, its wranglings and its obsessive quality it would not appeal to Hatch. It is not his way of doing things.

Although things can get rough in the South China Sea, and Hatch has perfected many manoeuvres to throw rivals off his trail, using both muscular and mental agility, they are not nearly as cut-throat as the operations off Florida. This is partly because Hatch is the only Singapore-based salvaging company to specialize in old wrecks: his competitors, who like him grew up on Second World War cargoes, have since they became unprofitable largely moved on to other work, principally oil explorations. But in Florida treasure is still the great obsession.

It is not hard to see why. The Spanish galleons carried those items – gold, silver, jewels, weapons, artifacts – which are still the most valuable and sought after. It is estimated that at least eight billion dollars worth of gold and silver was transported to Spain from the New World. Storms, pirates and bad seamanship ensured that thousands of vessels did not make the journey to Spain and most of these came to grief on the Florida Keys, which stretch for one hundred and fifty miles from Florida into the Gulf of Mexico.

With typical American vigour many of the most valuable cargoes have already been recovered: the *Atocha* was perhaps the last known monster hoard. But there is still a great deal of silver, and some gold, to be salvaged. For the men undertaking the work it is safer but less rewarding than in the "wild west" days of the 1950s and 1960s, before the Florida Government became alarmed, not only at the loss of potential state revenue from the wrecks, but at the fights and feuds that continually broke out.

Art McKee, the father, if not the grandfather, of the hunting, had been lifting cannon since the 1930s, and his company, Continental Exploration, was competing with Fisher to find the *Atocha*. McKee can tell of fights under water with rival gangs of divers. As they rounded on him, knives flashing, he managed to disperse them with a blast from his underwater shot gun, which he carried to scare off sharks.

Another of the old characters was Tom Gurr, who fell foul of the State authorities. He located the *San José*, one of the vessels in the 1733 silver fleet wrecked off Plantation Key, but was forced to hand over his finds to the Government. A battle in the courts went on for years, and finally Gurr, his patience exhausted, took up all the gold and silver he still retained and dumped it back into the sea over the wreck site.

Many of those salvaging in those days were ex-Servicemen, looking for the excitement in peace that they had experienced during the Second World War. They had little time for history, for careful excavation, for research: they followed hunches and rumours, and enjoyed sabotaging each other's boats, stealing treasure from a rival gang, and getting involved in underwater knife fights. When the Government began to bring law and order to this rough-house, it united the treasure hunters against it, and as much fun was to be had tricking the authorities. Undoubtedly much useful historical data was destroyed and many wrecks were badly salvaged. But the waters around Florida can also be regarded as the last American frontier.

Today the old hunters have been joined by the footloose young. It is all rather tame and much more professional. There are museums scattered over the State, catering for tourists. They show off the finds of the various salvaging companies; Fisher helped to finance his long search for the *Atocha* from sales of novelty merchandise from his replica of a Spanish galleon, the *Golden Doubloon*, where he presents his finds. Art McKee displays his collection of coins and cannon in an imitation castle. And the actual sites of the wrecks become a focus for tourists who gaze reflectively into the waters which were so recently squabbled over.

Apart from the Spanish treasure fleets, there are many other prizes – the scattered Armada around the UK; the thousands of antique vessels that went down in the Mediterranean in classical times, loaded with pots that are now avidly collected; and the individual ships, such as the *Lutine*, which sank off the Dutch coast in 1779, with bullion to pay the troops fighting Napoleon. Its bell was salvaged and sent to Lloyds of London, which had insured the cargo for a colossal £1.2 million. Today the *Lutine* bell is rung every time a ship goes missing, a dread toll for many, but a clarion, like the boxing bell at the start of a round, for many salvagers.

Few of the professional salvagers will have recouped their vast investment in underwater searches. Hatch has been the most consistently successful. As time goes by, it is the biggest operators, with the greatest financial backing, who will have the field to themselves. There will always be the chance of some small pickings for the week-end aqua club members, diving their local rocks and shallows; but the time needed for a conscientious, well-equipped and well-researched expedition is very expensive to buy.

What will be the next wreck to seize the public imagination? The successful attempts in 1986 to film the *Titanic* as she lies two miles down in the freezing waters of the North Atlantic have raised hopes that one day her cargo might be raised, but the equipment to salvage her is not yet up to the monumental task. The *Titanic*, like the challenge of space travel, exists to test man's resolve and capabilities rather than to offer any guaranteed commercial satisfaction.

But it is likely that the next headlines may come from the discovery of a long-lost but not quite forgotten hoard – such as the fleet of Kubla Khan. In 1279 this fabled character set out to plunder Japan with a vast armada. A storm wrecked his plans off the coast of Honshu and a priceless hoard of coins, weapons and porcelain waits to be recovered – one day.

Hatch has greatly extended the potential market for underwater finds – suddenly pots are as worth finding as gold bars. The salerooms, too, are playing their part in promoting a new field of collecting: underwater works of art. In the last five years Christie's Amsterdam saleroom has handled eight wrecks, disposing of twenty-two silver bars, ducatoons and artifacts from the Dutch East Indiaman *Slot ter Hooge*; coins and artifacts from the *Hollandia*, which fetched very high prices because the ship had been the flagship of the national hero Piet Heyns; Spanish and Dutch coins from the *Utrecht*; uncut emeralds and pre-Columbia gold jewellery from the *Nuestra Senora de Esperanza*, a Spanish galleon; pieces-of-eight from the British frigate *Athenienne*, and Portuguese coins from another wreck – all before Hatch came along with the junk and the "G".

Sotheby's is keen to hit back. It held its first auction of treasure, from British waters, as long ago as 1969 when it disposed of 2,000 coins, plate, jewels and guns from the controversial Scillies wreck, the *Association*. In all, it brought in over £20,000. But it would dearly love to hold an auction on the Nanking scale. It would require great marketing skills to present the coins, ingots and other artifacts from the *Atocha* with the same bravura that Christie's sold the Nanking, but Americans love a hero, and they love their past, and Sotheby's in New York will certainly have sounded out Fisher on whether he has considered disposing of his share of his loot in this way. Suddenly the sea bed is fashionable.

8

Political Matters

Immediately after the sale in Amsterdam, Hatch returned to Singapore. It is his base rather than his home – his real home is his comfortably fitted-out cabin of the *Restless M* – but Singapore has been good to him over the past seventeen years. He has now actually acquired an apartment there which he uses sometimes. It came in useful in the autumn of 1986 when his ship, while being given an overhaul and fitted with yet more navigational equipment, was struck by lightning in the dockyard. But as soon as possible he was back on board and out to sea, prospecting his next wreck.

But although he is at the very peak of his profession, the most famous salvage expert in the world, his success has brought him problems. He is now, thanks to his high profile, a marked man. He has to battle on two fronts in particular – with Governments and with the academic establishment. Hatch's way of doing things – his "up and at 'em" approach to life – inevitably risks confrontation with authority.

For example, the very perfection of his find when he came across the *Geldermalsen* has brought him much criticism from historians and scholars.

On his next major operation Hatch is open to the suggestion that a marine archaeologist accompanies him. Hatch is not averse to fame and rather likes the idea of a permanent record of his achievements. He compares his contribution to knowledge – by getting up and doing it – with that of the academics, theorizing from the safety of their studies. And he thinks he achieves more.

Hatch has to take the academics seriously because they have the ear of Governments and could make his job impossible. There are moves afoot in many countries to make all discovered wrecks the property of the State, protected areas until historians have the time and the money to explore them. This is the case in Australia where treasure hunting has almost disappeared. If you find a wreck you can earn a small reward from reporting its location but excavation is undertaken by historians, such as Jeremy Green, director of the Museum of Marine Archaeology in Freemantle. He says, "There is nothing more tragic than seeing sites which have been smashed up and ships' timbers broken and

Hatch – as seen by the Financial Times.

destroyed." Five East Indiamen suffered summary rape by wreck pirates in Western Australia before the State stepped in in 1970 to protect them.

It is only in recent years, thanks to the new diving equipment, that wrecks have become available to a new generation of commercial divers. When salvagers made their living from recovering the cargo of Second World War ships, and other recent victims of the sea, it hardly mattered if they dynamited the vessels to bits: indeed, that was the basic approach. Suddenly the growing interest in archaeology

confronts head-on the initiatives of men like Hatch in the exploration
of the past.

Archaeologists are turning increasingly to the sea for new and
important finds. Water can preserve organic remains, like food, clothes
and wood, better than they would survive on land, and an intact wreck
is a much more interesting time-capsule of the past than any built-over
archaeological site, except perhaps an unexcavated tomb. But the
expense and time it takes to excavate a wreck in the academic way was
revealed in the *Mary Rose* venture, the recovery of a Tudor warship
from Portsmouth harbour, which took many years and many millions.

There is a real conflict of interest. Without men like Hatch there
would be few new discoveries – university departments do not have the
guts, funds or time to mount many highly speculative expeditions. But
Hatch can only work in a free market. If Draconian laws take away the
liberty of the salvagers to venture where they will, illegal activities and
much personal rancour follow. Mediterranean countries forbid
collecting from the sea bed, with the result that few important
treasures surface, and a great deal of illicit trading in small and
insignificant items persists. And there are many frustrated divers.

The academic moves slowly, carefully, methodically, with a
programme over many seasons. Hatch has to recover as much as
possible as quickly as possible, preferably in one season, before rivals
infringe on the site, and costs escalate out of the control of even very
wealthy individuals and into the realms of red-tape-bound institutions
and governments. He cannot spend time marking down the location of
every single object on a wreck, in three dimensions. On the "G" he did
a rough archaeological survey, and John Bremmer's pictures provided
useful data. But photographs also played into the hands of Hatch's
critics. One shot shows a diver prising open a chest, while a plank
disappears into the deep. On the plank are Chinese characters.
Historians would dearly like to know the exact text of that inscription.

The only solution is compromise. If the public had to choose, it
would probably side with the freebooting attitude of Hatch and his like
– the explorers, the risk-takers, the creators, the achievers. But the
educated minority point to the two million visitors who go to see the
re-salvaged *Mary Rose*, and say that once-in-a-life-time opportunities
for historical knowledge are being sacrificed for a quick financial return.

Hatch would like to work with the academic establishment. He
co-operated fully with Dr Christiaan Jorg, the leading Dutch historian
on the trade with the Far East in the seventeenth and eighteenth
centuries, to mutual benefit. Jorg's research, based on Hatch's finds,
proved conclusively that the wreck was the *Geldermalsen*. This
provided a great deal of new information about the actual trade in the

Oumepouder | Vhoffe of vzon Vhoffe of Glory | Souxe Roth

The Mary Rose in 1536. She sank off Portsmouth and was excavated with attention to scholarship.

mid-eighteenth century between the Netherlands and the orient – and also increased the publicity and the value of Hatch's and Max's find. It was a fair exchange. Hatch and his partners are always generous in gifts to museums, notably those in Singapore and the Netherlands, who have displays of porcelain from his wrecks, as well as more monumental objects, such as the bell from the "G."

Obviously, from an historian's point of view, the activities of some of the more brash salvagers are almost criminal. Valuable evidence is wantonly destroyed, the perfect discovery of the intact past is thoughtlessly trampled upon. Wrecks are turned over to see if they contain valuables and then abandoned. But co-operating with academics is too frustrating and too expensive to appeal to many search companies. Inevitably Governments are stepping in to decide the conflict between the pursuit of knowledge on the one hand, and on the other the infringement of personal liberties and the risk of no more worthwhile discoveries.

Hatch and Max are proud of the way they "dived" the "G." They used non-destructive techniques. The tea and the sand were removed by airlift; the porcelain was recovered almost in its entirety; no part of the remains of the hull were destroyed. No explosives were used. An archaeological dig of the *Geldermalsen* would still be worthwhile.

Sunken treasure from ships of the Spanish Armada was studied and raised by historians.

The US Government has recently passed legislation covering its Outer Continental Shelf, under which oil companies, when prospecting there, have to spend a percentage of their total investment budget on an archaeological site survey so that their operations are not destroying any antiquities. After a difficult transition, the salvagers of Florida have learned to co-operate with the State.

What is the actual position of the law? It varies very much from country to country. In the UK the Merchant Shipping Acts of 1894 and 1906 require anyone finding anything on a wreck to pass it over to the nearest Receiver of Wrecks. If they can prove they own the wreck, or the salvage rights to it, they can hold on to their discoveries. Even if they have no such advantages they can benefit from their enterprise if no-one turns up to claim the objects found within a year.

The boom in treasure hunting in the last twenty-five years has produced more legislation in the UK. In 1973 the Protection of Wrecks Act was passed, which enables the Government to declare a wreck a protected area, at the same time licensing an appointed specialist salvager to work the site and punishing any interlopers. So far only thirty wrecks off the British coast have been found worthy of "historical, archaeological and artistic importance", and thus gain protection, and the slow process of academic investigation is underlined by the fact that only one of the thirty, the *Mary Rose*, has been the subject of an intensive excavation. So far the Government has put out markers, but they have produced few tangible benefits, for salvagers or historians.

If Governments become too restrictive, the effects will inevitably lead to illicit dealing in underwater treasures. Already there are rumours that not all the bullion was officially lifted from the *Edinburgh*, and that much of the gold and plate which was declared to be on the *Association* failed to reach the open market. Co-operation between salvagers and the authorities, between men like Hatch and the academic world, is essential.

Unfortunately many archaeologists refuse to work with salvage companies. They find their concern with profit unattractive: if they had their way no treasures would be sold off for commercial gain, only saved for posterity in museums. Hatch has had to become a diplomat to deal with the enemies of his profession. He says he has to balance the demands of the archaeologists with his loyalty to his financial backers and the men who work for him. But in the end he holds the trump cards. It is only his bravery and initiative that make the finds possible. Unless he can dispose of any valuables he recovers on the market, he will not continue. And there will be fewer breakthroughs in underwater archaeological knowledge. It is a clash of temperaments – the professional salvager is likely to be a much more wordly and adventurous character than a professional academic, with his belief in detail and study.

But there are now signs that the leading divers are prepared to do deals with the authorities. In Florida the State has benefitted to the tune of many millions of dollars from the cut it takes from recovered wrecks, and in the UK divers such as Rex Cowan increasingly co-operate with officialdom. It can bring benefits. Cowan made an agreement with the Dutch Government, which claims to be the heir of the Dutch East India Company, in his salvaging of the *Hollandia*, off the Scillies. The Dutch got twenty-five per cent of any commercial finds and Cowan got the right to dive for the wreck. However this official title did not stop him being the target of a petrol bomb from a rival team: it wrecked his search boat.

Hatch also came to a deal with the Dutch Government over the *Geldermalsen*, but was able to persuade it to take just ten per cent because of the costs of the salvaging and the fact that the wreck was many thousands of miles away from the Netherlands. But his negotiations with the Dutch awakened the interest of the Indonesian

Government and, in future, Hatch is keen to work in partnership with this heir to the many islands of the Dutch East Indies.

The location of the *Geldermalsen* raised complex issues over ownership. By proving it was a Dutch East Indiamen, Hatch attracted the attention of the authorities in the Netherlands. But he could hardly keep its origins secret; nor would he want to do so: the Dutch became his ally in the excavation. But the site of the wreck, although not in Indonesian territorial waters, was in Indonesia's exclusive economic zone which, as defined by the united Nations Convention on the Law of the Sea, covers oil and other materials, but makes no reference to wrecks.

It is not in Hatch's interests to be a thorn in the side of the Indonesians. He well knows there are many choice wrecks definitely in their territorial waters. As he found with the Malaysian Government, in his salvage of the *Risdam*, co-operation is much more profitable than conflict. It has taken the Indonesian Government time to appreciate the potential value of the wrecks of European (as well as local) ships in its waters, but the £10 million Hatch raised at the Amsterdam sale has concentrated its mind wonderfully. Hatch would like to have the contract to investigate all the most likely wrecks in the coastal strip. He has prepared a schedule. In return the Indonesians would share any profits from finds.

The Indonesians need the help of professionals such as Hatch. The major tragedy in the hunt for the *Geldermalsen* was the death of a young Indonesian marine archaeologist, one of only five in the country, who went missing when diving on the site of the wreck during an official Indonesian mission in late August 1986. It is to be hoped that this sad event will bond the relationship between Hatch and the Indonesians.

Undoubtedly the £10 million raised so publicly at auction has alerted the Governments of the world to the financial possibilities from the archaeological remains in their territorial waters which, since the UN Convention on the Law of the Sea in 1982, are legally under their jurisdiction. Hatch has been flooded with offers from Governments to sell them his skills. One offer is from Colombia, where another great, treasure-laden, Spanish galleon lies waiting in deep waters.

In the past Hatch has been happiest in the area he knows best – the South China Sea. He knows the waters; the risks; the politics; the competitors; the likely finds. But just as he felt that the Second World War cargoes in the far East were played out so he is now tempted by wider horizons. He likes to undertake some research himself in the various maritime record offices in London, Amsterdam and elsewhere, and he still has Henri Besancon working with him. He is amazed that more historians, especially those without a job, do not try and ferret out likely leads: he is always open to suggestions, and Besancon has become a wealthy man through his assistance to Hatch.

Of course all the easy targets, the famous ships with valuable cargoes which went down in shallow waters close to coasts, have been explored. But often the expeditions mounted even ten years ago lacked the equipment to do a thorough job. While Hatch plans his next major venture, there are always opportunities for fun-diving on old wrecks, well-loved favourites. There are many reefs like the Admiral Stellingwerf within a day's sailing of Singapore.

There will always be an uneasy relationship between Hatch and historians, between Hatch and Governments. He is a professional salvager; they are both after something very different from under-water wrecks, although Third World States, after the Amsterdam auction, may well put financial return before historical recovery. As he showed in his negotiations with the Dutch Government over the "G", Hatch can talk to officials and academics and agree deals. It could well be that the era of freebooting the seas is over, at least in territorial waters. But few controls operate over international waters. There are fewer wrecks out there, many miles from land, and they may be much harder to locate and to salvage, but the eyes of the professional operators are looking in that direction as controls threaten to inhibit diving in more accessible waters.

9

The Next Wreck

What sort of man is Michael Hatcher?

To a great extent he is just what you would expect, given his life story. From the start he has been forced to stand on his own two feet – at Dr Barnardo's, at farm school in Australia, on the road selling, sailing round the world, competing with other divers over wrecks, taking on Governments. He is a character out of the *Boys Own Paper*: a rugged individualist, a man's man, a hater of authority, a believer in hard work and personal initiative. The combination of Yorkshire blood and Australian young manhood could hardly produce any other type. He was dealt an awful hand of cards at birth and look what he has done with the deck? He has little sympathy with whiners and piners.

He has a simple political philosophy. Governments are representatives, on trust to the people. They should announce what they are going to do, and if, after a year, they have not kept to their pledges they should be out, paying some forfeit for failing to deliver their deal with the nation.

Yet there is also something slightly vulnerable about him. He is aware that there are other worlds about which he knows little and he is keen to learn about them. The way he has thrown himself into studying Chinese porcelain is remarkable. He is not yet an expert, but he is quite prepared to argue with the specialists. He respects knowledge, but appreciates character more. He had his battles with Christie's, a company populated with a very different type of person from Hatch, but quickly came to trust some of the executives, while having no time at all for those he considered to be bullshitters.

He has a great loyalty to his crew but he firmly controls the divers. He has been known to administer the bank accounts of some of the Malaysian divers to stop them squandering their money too quickly. He himself has no great love of wealth. It has hardly changed his life. He travels at the front end of the aircraft now and buys himself an expensive meal when he fancies one – often Japanese cuisine – but he certainly does not dress like a millionaire. When in London he quickly moved out of the Ritz to a modest hotel near Richmond. He did not like the fact that he had to wear a tie for dinner at the Ritz – he did not have a tie. Luckily in Singapore dress is casual; on the *Restless M* it is virtually non-existent.

Max and Hatch, partners in adventure.

He is a very tough man and physically strong. At forty-six, many have given up diving: Hatch still loves it. He is at his happiest on board his boat. It is not a luxurious craft, no sleek white motor launch, rather a black, well-worn, work-horse of a boat. He has invested some of the money he made from the Nanking cargo in yet better radar and communications equipment but, while the saloon is comfortable, and it is fun on the promenade deck where a line enables you to fish at will while the ship idles, the only really comfortable cabin is Hatch's, with its large bed, its mementoes of his triumphs (including a cartoon of him as a pirate piloting the porcelain to Christie's), and its wall maps.

He is well advised by Ong on his money, and has bought property in the United States and Australia, as well as the Singapore apartment. He owns shares which he worries about; his daily spending is negligible. His one rule of life is, "I'm not allowed to sell real estate to look for treasure."

He also buys old sea charts and maps, and antique navigational equipment. There is his porcelain collection; after a burglary on his boat he sold much of it, but he still has some very choice items.

He is self-taught in most things – in diving, in sailing, in salvaging, in engineering. He would be the best possible man to have with you if you fancied a treck across Antarctica or over the Gobi Desert. He is afraid of no man, but aware that some will have advantages – social, intellectual – that he must watch out for. He quickly sizes them up and makes up his mind, according to his own scale of judgement. He believes that he is at the very top of his profession and he cannot imagine a better one. The discovery of historical wrecks has given him a new lease of life: he was bored with salvaging modern cargoes. He has made his money from that. Now he wants something a little more exciting.

You would think that Hatch had had enough excitement in his life already. He is fond of telling mind-boggling stories only to add, "You must never repeat that. One day, perhaps, when I'm dead." He has undoubtedly made enemies, and life is still cheap in South East Asia. There are rivals in the region who would break open the champagne bottles if Hatch were wiped out. He is not the type of man to turn the other cheek, and his memories of shoot-outs and knife battles suggest the eighteenth century rather than the twentieth. But then the South China Sea, with its Thai pirates and Vietnamese boat people, its rich cargoes and weak navies, is the last great untamed stretch of water in the world.

To have reached the top there you have to be very sharp and very ruthless. There are often sudden flurries of action in the bars in Singapore port which leave men dead, killed in drunken brawls over gold rings or women. Yet Hatch has survived. Now he is moving into a new world – of international celebrity, of appearances on television programmes, of meetings with Government ministers and corporate bosses (there have been enquiries, after the Nanking sale, from American corporations wondering whether United Subsea Services was for sale). Hatch seems to cope with the change in his lifestyle easily: by not changing at all. He is still restive when confined to his office; he is still champing to get out to sea.

Even on holiday Hatch is active, rushing off on ten-mile wind-surfer races, or following up local rumours of a wreck in the neighbourhood. Going out with him for the day on such a hunt gives a good indication of his working life. So much of it is routine, Max sitting motionless over the side-scan sonar, not reacting as other crew members draw his attention to changes in colour or odd shapes on the print-out – he knows that they are just rocks or coral. For hours the *Restless M* purrs over expanses of ocean only limited by the distant skyline. You think – how can anything be found in such a vast space? Hatch is restless, moving from the bridge to talk to local fishermen – who invariably know where the wrecks are – testing out his diving gear. Eventually, to keep the divers happy, a possible spot is selected and over the side they go, anxious to get under water. On this occasion the haul was an old anchor and two fish, but the monotony had been broken, the sea had been breached.

Hatch shares one other characteristic with the Victorian Empire builders: a respect for women. He has never been married but has devoted his life to looking after his younger sister, who now lives in Australia. He has had many girlfriends and currently has a happy relationship with Ghislaine, whom he met when she worked as a diplomat in the British High Commission in Singapore. She organizes his life when he is on land and has found an interesting and potentially profitable niche in the company by making jewellery from shards from the Nanking. The small pieces of blue and white porcelain make the perfect centrepieces for rings, brooches, lockets, when set off in gold.

"Nanking jewellery". Ghislaine looks after the marketing of this attractive accessory from the wreck.

Negotiations are well advanced to make and market the Nanking jewellery range. Now Ghislaine and Michael Hatcher are engaged to be married.

Hatch is aware of the other commercial spin-offs from his great find. He would never again lose control of the rights to the film of any enterprise, as he did the Nanking with the BBC. His next major trip could have the makings of a fascinating feature film. He also sees the possibilities in promotional merchandise.

Hatch is in no doubt that he salvaged the *Geldermalsen* because Max threw his time, equipment and money into the chase: Max actually found the wreck. He is the perfect foil to Hatch, a quiet, rumpled giant who holds Hatch back on his more hare-brained schemes, but who is also infected by the need for action. They are always competing with each other – at backgammon and on their surf-boards. Max has moved his side-scan sonar and his magnetometer on to Hatch's boat. It looks like the start of a long partnership, although they will continue to undertake individual missions. Max has a wife, Mary; a home aboard a junk in Hong Kong; and children to educate. He has roots. But as Hatch tries to tempt him on another trip – "Let's go and check that wreck on the Nicobars, Max" – "I know of a beach which is full of broken porcelain. There must be something there, Max" – "You'll like diving off Malaysia, Max" – 'you can see de Rham wrestling between his cautious, thinking, calculating half, and his speculating, excitement-hungry, adventurous half.

Hatch has undeniably been lucky in finding two valuable wrecks. The ships that disappeared far out at sea are undetectable with current equipment, and undivable, too. Most wrecks are close to shore and well known to professional salvagers. But many will be lost for ever under the sea bed, or be smashed to pieces, or be already looted. Few professional salvagers make a worthwhile living, and most of the speculative companies set up to plumb the seas have proved a very bad investment: many have gone bankrupt. You can be the most skilled, the most brave, the most tenacious, the best briefed diver in the world, but without luck you will have a hard, disappointing career. You also have to be able to negotiate with fickle, nervous, and sometimes venal third world Governments.

Hatch has one great advantage over his competitors: his track record has brought him time, money and international fame. He can take his time; invest his money in even better equipment – there is talk of a video to film under the sea, and a machine which even in the darkest water gives the divers "impressions" of objects; and when he does find another wreck he will have no problems marketing it.

What of the future? By late 1986 the *Restless M* was already at sea again, re-fitted and repaired, and fully primed to undertake another expedition. The local monsoons determine what parts of the ocean can be explored at particular times of the year, and in the months around Christmas only the area to the west of Singapore, up the Malacca Straits and into the Indian Ocean is worth investigating. So Hatch was off, partly for pleasure but always with a list of sites that might just be worth diving. But he has reached the stage in his career where freebooting is over. In future the serious operations will be well researched, well planned, and with the agreement of Governments, or other possible owners of any wrecks discovered.

There is a long list of possibilities. There are the approaches from Colombia to advise on the Spanish galleon, but it is in very deep water, so deep that its salvaging would involve new diving techniques and a very long and expensive search. Max has a fancy to return to the sea of his youth – the Mediterranean, rich in wrecks but well controlled by Governments.

It is more than likely that Hatch will keep to the seas of South East Asia. The Malaysian Government would like a thorough salvage of the *Risdam* and areas where there are still many valuable objects to be recovered, including much eighteenth-century Thai porcelain, as well as timber. There could well be a contract, covering many wrecks. There is talk of a wreck off the Nicobars, an attractive area to dive. Every month new leads arrive in Singapore; new reports from fishermen who have come up with a pot or a coin; new discoveries, in the archives, of ships that went down with valuable cargoes. Hatch now sits at the centre of a vast mass of data, weighing up the possibilities. It has become a problem; his amazing success in finding two such different, two such worthwhile, wrecks, both in historical and commercial terms, has imposed a burden on him. The next Hatch find must be of equal importance to maintain his reputation.

In the Netherlands Henri Besancon chases up the surviving data on the sixty vessels missing on the trip from China to Europe, or vice versa, in the two centuries after 1650. All the team are well aware that it was a miracle, the combination of the tea on top, and the slow descent beneath a cover of protective sand, that enabled the *Geldermalsen* porcelain to survive. There are perhaps six or seven possibilities among the lost Dutch East Indiamen, but the majority of these went down in deep water. Henry has a short list of two, perhaps three which could prove worthwhile projects, but their exact position has yet to be determined.

There are rumours that Hatch has found another site, and judging by the one dish that he has taken from the sea there it could provide a most wonderful treble. For it is a green-glazed celadon dish of the mid-fourteenth century, Yuan porcelain that complements, pat, the seventeenth-century blue and white Ming from the junk, and the eighteenth-century Chinese export porcelain from the *Geldermalsen*. He is obviously giving little away about his new discovery. The plate was found in very dark water, very close to Indonesia. Any salvage operation would be with the co-operation of the Indonesian Government, which would share in the financial rewards, and allocate important finds to its national museums. Tough negotiations and a difficult diving challenge await Hatch.

In the end, if there is a junk on the sea bed, the likelihood is that most of its cargo will have been smashed to pieces over the centuries. For ceramics of this period to have survived would be a miracle. But, on the evidence of the one dish, this would be a find that would have the connoisseurs of Chinese works of art buzzing with excitement. Whatever happens Hatch, will come up with something. He has the bit between his teeth. By his courage, enterprise, skill and good fortune he has become the most successful underwater venturer of our, or any, generation. He has the time and the money to amaze the world again; and he also has the will to do so.

Acknowledgements

The author would like to acknowledge with gratitude the great help he received in preparing this book from Mark Wrey and Colin Sheaf of Christie's; David Howard of Heirloom & Howard; Rex Cowan; Henri Besancon; and of course Mike Hatcher and Max de Rham.

The publishers would like also to acknowledge their debt of gratitude to Michael Hatcher and Max de Rham, and their very warm thanks to John Bremmer and Christie's Fine Art for the many photographs they so generously supplied.

Thanks also to Henri Besancon for research and photographs relating to Captain Hatcher's salvaging operations; to Axel Vervoordt, in particular for his help with photographs of the Ming treasures; to David Howard of Heirloom & Howard, for his assistance and his generosity; to Dr C. J. A. Jorg, author of *The Geldermalsen, History & Porcelain*, for his help with historical photographs; to Rex Cowan of Worlds Edge Films for the photographs of his own and other divers' finds; to Colin Sheaf of Christie's London, for his cooperation and support; to Hetti Jongsma and Anita André de la Porte of Christie's Amsterdam, for kind assistance; to Gerald Cinamon of Cinamon and Kitzinger for design.

Unless listed below by page number, all photographs are by John Bremmer or Max de Rham or by kind permission of Christie's Fine Art. The publishers thank the following:

Dr Barnardo's, page 58.
Martin Paternotte, pages 66, 67, 68 and 69.
Axel Vervoordt, Antwerp, pages 72, 74, 78, 83 and 84.
Heirloom & Howard, pages 77 and 133.
Dr C. J. A. Jorg (from his book, *The Geldermalsen, History and Porcelain*), page 89.
Algemeen Rijksarchief, The Hague: pages 90 and 91 (from Collection Rademacher 98); page 93 (from Archive Canton Factory, 140, documents 1773).
Rijksarchief in Zeeland, Middelburg, page 92 (from Collection Zelandia Illustrata II-460).
Trustees of the Victoria & Albert Museum, pages 94 below and 98-9.
Collection Groninger Museum, Groningen, page 92.
Osterreichische Nationalbibliothek, Vienna, page 100.
Princessehof Museum, Leeuarden, page 103.
Harrods, page 135.
Maurice Hyams & Elisabeth C. Porter, page 136.
The Ritz Hotel, London, page 138.
Worlds Edge Films, pages 143, 144, 145, 149, 150 above and 154 below.
Paul Armiger, page 150 below (supplied by Worlds Edge Films).
Peter Marsden, page 151 (supplied by Worlds Edge Films).

Syd Jones, page 154 above (supplied by Worlds Edge Films).
Michael Daley, page 161.
The Master and Fellows of Magdalene College, Cambridge, page 163.
Colin Martin, page 164.
Robert Glenn Ltd, page 171.

The photographs on pages 47, 48 and 55 include seventeenth-century porcelain.